HARPOONS

HARPOONS

ARTHUR ROSENFELD

A Delta Book
Published by
Dell Publishing
a division of
Bantam Doubleday Dell Publishing Group, Inc.
666 Fifth Avenue
New York, New York 10103

Library of Congress Cataloging in Publication Data

Rosenfeld, Arthur.
Harpoons.

I. Title.
PS3568.0812H37   1989   813'.54   88-33573
ISBN 0-385-29732-7

Printed in the United States of America
Published simultaneously in Canada
June 1989

10 9 8 7 6 5 4 3 2 1
BG

For Arline,
who keeps the world at bay

1

When Scooter Loon was stolen he was too young to focus his eyes. He was also sensitive to noises, and the world seemed very loud to his virgin ears.

Scooter Loon's foster parents had no other children. In fact, they were lucky to have Scooter. Scooter's adopted father was a cat burglar, and as such knew some wildly creative positions, but try as he would, copulating with Scooter's mother at secret and frequent intervals, he could not successfully join sperm with egg.

"The doctor assures me that I'm normal," said Scooter's mom, Marian, in her own defense.

"The doctor assures me I've harpoons aplenty," lied Roman Loon, who was in fact as sterile as cold rice.

"Maybe we're doing it wrong," said Marian.

Roman Loon knew that their technique was laudable, because despite his depleted tanks, he was doing it many, many times a week with women all over town.

Roman fancied himself a Brit of ages gone by, when the cadre of cat burglars in London was an elite group. There was a tradition and a code of ethics, Roman often explained to his wife, and many things one could and could not do. Often, when Roman was climbing rooftops and scuttling down drainpipes, he longed for a son with whom he could share his exploits. He wanted desperately to be respected, but he insisted upon being a crook.

The lead to Scooter came from a gang of baby thieves, low-life riffraff with whom Roman Loon associated upon occasion. A man despairing of his masculinity is a ship in desperate waters, however, and Roman was willing to take virtually any course that might net him a boy. Mostly the baby gang stole from Mexican households down south in Chula Vista and other border towns where poor whites mingled with border overspill. The baby gang found that while poor people got violent and desperate about the loss of their children, and would occasionally shoot a gang member full of holes where he froze in their homes, they lacked the financial wherewithal to command either private eyes, lawyers, or the attention of the police.

Periodically, though, the gang would get cocky and go for the newborn child of a socialite or family of means. From the business standpoint such babies brought little extra profit and lots of extra trouble, but baby thieves don't have stockbroker minds, and the sheer risk was sometimes impetus enough.

Scooter, whose given name was Bernard, was born to the wife of a successful Jewish lawyer who lived in a large, white, porticoed house in the Bel Air section of Los Angeles. Sharon, Scooter's natural mother, had beautiful, thick auburn hair that had grown in both length and luster during her pregnancy due to the special attention she paid to her diet. Scooter's natural father, Adam, was a tall and handsome man who wore small, round, wire-rimmed glasses that made him look bookish. He took his glasses off only when he showered and played squash. He left them on while asleep on airplanes and during intimate encounters with Sharon, claiming he liked to be able to look at her while they made love. He was wearing them the night Bernard, later Scooter, was conceived.

Adam was the type of man who liked everything to be "just so." While he was thrilled to have a son, he was appalled by the fact that his cringing, screaming, red-faced little Bernard had six fingers on his right hand and six toes on his left foot. The doctor who delivered Scooter had gone to Yale with Adam, and he knew just how the wealthy lawyer felt. He liked things a certain way too.

"Can't you cut them off, now while he's small and doesn't have much feeling?" asked Scooter's biological dad.

"Don't be silly," said the doctor. "I'm not a veterinarian and these aren't Doberman ears."

Incredibly it was this same doctor who was ultimately responsible for the theft of Bernard. The doctor had a large-breasted, attractive assistant named Clea, who was as infertile as Roman Loon. As neurotically fearful of paternity suits as gynecologists are wont to be, this woman's presence made the doctor desire incarnate. He took Clea in the copy room, in the envelope closet, and between patients on the crisp tissue paper of the examining room, with the stirrups pushed wide. This level of intimacy between doctor and nurse allowed few secrets between them, and the doctor knew that the object of his affections was married to the leader of the baby gang. After giving the matter much thought, the doctor broached the matter of the deformed Steinberg child.

"I don't really think that Mr. Steinberg wants the baby," said the doctor.

"What about the mother?" asked Clea slyly as she ran her hands through the doctor's thick chest hair.

"I'm sure she's not too pleased with the child either."

Clea's heart sang, for she hated all women who could squeeze children out from between their loins as easily as wet grapes through fingers. She reserved extra-special hate for Sharon because she was not only fertile but rich.

"It would not be a terrible thing, then, if something were to happen to the baby?"

"If something were to happen"—the doctor groaned slightly as the nurse's hands ran low—"the baby would have to end up far, far from here. He is, after all, quite easy to identify."

"I understand," said the nurse.

It was a fine measure of the contrast between Roman Loon and Adam Steinberg that the cat burglar was entranced by the baby-gang leader's description of Bernard. More fingers to burgle with, more toes to climb with, thought Roman, promptly determining to heist the child himself.

In a subconscious sign of distaste for his infant son, Adam Steinberg decided that Scooter would not be allowed to sleep in his parents' bedroom, even though he was still sucking incessantly on his mother's nipple. Adam issued this edict one night after a grueling day in court.

Sharon went berserk. "What the hell's the matter with you!" she cried. "This is our little boy! Haven't you ever heard of crib death? Haven't you ever heard of a baby starving? Haven't you heard about what happens to babies that are left alone, how they grow up with strange and twisted personalities and hate people? Haven't you heard of baby thieves?"

Adam Steinberg shook his head wearily. "I just can't stand the crying and yelping all night," he said. "I have to get up and go to work in the morning. You can stay home and nap. You can give the meals and the shopping over to the cook or the maid. I need to have my rest."

"I can't believe this is happening," sobbed Sharon.

She would never have used up that phrase if she had known what was going to happen next.

It was the kind of night that Roman Loon liked best for working. A hot and dry September night in L.A., when the Santa Ana winds rolled in and dried everything to the cracking point. Roman liked such nights because they were so full of sounds. Shutters and windows rattled and palm trees and cockroaches hissed. On these nights homebodies became inured to little creaks and scrapings, assuming them to be the weather's work.

Roman the cat burglar reached the Bel Air home of Adam and Sharon Steinberg at approximately three fifteen in the morning. He dropped low behind a parked car and checked the pencil scrawl on a little piece of paper with a red-tipped flashlight. Certain that he had the right address, he circled the house twice looking for signs of an alarm system or guard dog. He found neither.

Because of both earthquake peril and the plenitude of land early on, most houses in California are long and low. The Steinbergs' house was an exception, having both a second floor and an attic. As much for the drama of it as anything else, Roman Loon decided to penetrate the house from the top.

Extracting a white nylon cord that had been dyed deep blue, the thief attached a grappling hook and tossed it high. It landed with a dull thud behind the chimney, a gratuitous fixture in the southland but one upon which Sharon had insisted. Wrapping his feet around the drainpipe that faced the backyard, Roman shimmied himself expertly up to a small attic window, taped and broke the glass, and entered the first house of the son he was about to steal. The criminal was not bedazzled by the fact that the Steinbergs' rejected furniture was finer than the stuff he had stolen for his own home. His mind was steaming so with his quest that he did not even notice. He made his way softly down the attic stairs, wearing black basketball sneakers with bottoms dyed navy to match his rope. He found the door unlocked and opened it inch by inch. He found himself in the bedroom of Scooter Loon's natural sire and dam. He stared admiringly at Sharon's auburn tresses and evaluated the genitals of lawyer Adam as he lay revealed atop tousled sheets. In perhaps the truest of all testimonials to Roman's utter sociopathy, he felt not the slightest glimmer of guilt or remorse as he slunk by them and down the hall in search of his burgling heir.

Roman Loon was one lucky crook. As it happened Sharon had finished a nocturnal feeding session with Bernard a scant eight minutes before Roman's arrival. She was getting used to her somnambulant journeys down the hall and so was her baby. Sharon had drifted off into quick and deep sleep just as Roman opened the attic door.

Strapped to his back, Roman Loon wore a very special sack. It had begun as a small mountaineering bag, but the thief had modified it for the occasion, lining it with the cheap imitation sheepskin that is used on some car seats. Between the fleece and the nylon outer shell there was a layer of soundproofing material of the sort found beneath the ceiling panels of concert halls. There were air holes punched in the side, the fabric sewn flush and smooth by the loving hands of Marian Loon.

Bernard, later Scooter, lay in infant repose in a wooden cradle made of real ebony sent to Sharon upon her initial swelling by her mother in Wisconsin. Roman shrugged off his special backpack and lifted the tiny boy gently out of the crib. Scooter opened his unfocused eyes wide for the very first time, stared at Roman, and began to scream. Roman's gloved hands were trapped beneath the baby's armpits, so he did the only thing he could do—he covered Scooter's mouth with his own. Scooter's first vision, albeit fuzzy, was thus of the lean face of Roman the cat burglar, and his first French kiss was with a man who tasted like sardines.

Bernard's little chest heaved with moans as Roman bent over and half dropped him into the baby sack. The instant his hands were free, Loon secured the top zipper and smiled as he heard the tiny muffled squeaks that were the best bellows of the eleven-fingered boy. Creeping quietly back down the hall, Roman entered the master bedroom just as Sharon Steinberg stirred and rose to sit on the edge of her bed. The cat burglar froze, willing his shadow to melt in with the long dark block of the door. Those few moments, while Sharon's eyes were still open and Roman held his breath, with baby Bernard wriggling against the small of his back, were perhaps the longest in Loon's burgling career. Finally, Sharon rubbed her eyes, stretched her hands skyward, and collapsed back to the pillow. The baby thief counted to seventy-one, his lucky number, and crossed the room on tiptoe to the attic door.

Once in the attic, Roman was home free. He hopped through the window, grabbed the rope, and slid all but silently down to the fine-trimmed lawn. He was away and into his VW microbus before lawyer Adam awoke smiling from a dream.

2

Adam Steinberg stood by the curtains in his study and stared out the window at more police cars than he had thought existed west of the Rockies. Before moving into entertainment law and contracts, Adam had mingled with police and found them a thick-tongued and stony bunch. Now there were forensic specialists spreading white powder along his windowsills and nameless men in blue caps examining his social calender and appointment book. An FBI special agent named Niles Grosbeak sat on Adam's puffy white couch amid vast numbers of legal texts, journals, and art books. He was talking, but Adam was not listening. Instead he was examining his own feelings, wondering at the strong sense of relief he felt. Certainly a part of him worried about the little boy, but another part was glad to have his life "just so" again. Adam was enough of a man to realize that being relieved by the crime meant that there was something sad about his life, but he was also smart enough not to mention his feelings, particularly when the police were around.

Sharon had just been heavily sedated by the doctor and lay comatose in the bedroom. The special agent stopped talking as Sharon's doctor, the former Yale man, appeared in the doorway.

"I've given her a shot so she can rest," he announced. The doctor had in no way anticipated the magnitude of Sharon's anguish and, cold and superficial man that he was, he faced his own role in the affair with increasing alarm.

"It is preliminary for me to say," said the agent, "but I have an idea that this kidnapping may be the work of a gang of baby thieves that I have been tracking for some time. Do you have any thoughts, Doctor?"

"A rather farfetched idea in this day and age," said the gynecologist. "I would have thought that baby thieves went out with slaves and pirates."

"Not so," said Niles Grosbeak, peering at the doctor. "As last night's events indicate."

"Are you saying that organized criminals have my Bernard?" asked Adam Steinberg, suddenly aware of the conversation.

"This does seem to be the work of professionals," said the special agent. "No prints anywhere, an attic entry, skilled window taping and breakage—yes, I'm afraid those are all signs of experienced work."

"You're saying that they came in for the express purpose of kidnapping my son," said Adam.

"They didn't take anything else," the FBI man said.

"Perhaps they came in for silver and televisions and discovered the baby while they were poking around," ventured the doctor.

"Who pokes around for silver in a bedroom?" Adam Steinberg snapped.

"Maybe they were looking for jewelry," said the doctor.

"Jewel thieves rarely enter occupied houses," said Grosbeak. "What most interests me is how they knew there was a baby here. Does your wife walk about the neighborhood with the child in a carriage?"

"This is Bel Air. We don't do much sidewalk strolling here," said Adam.

"No, of course not," said the special agent. "What about shopping? Does your wife clothes-shop with the child?"

"She's only been home from the hospital a week," said Adam. "She hasn't done much shopping."

"Forgive my asking," said the G-man, "but this *is* Bel Air."

"Well at least he shouldn't be hard to identify," said Adam Steinberg.

"I'm afraid babies all look pretty much alike, unless of course they belong to you."

"Not my baby," said Adam, rocking back onto the couch and raising his hands and his feet in the air.

Any policeman will tell you that the longer a perpetrator remains at large, the more unlikely it is that he will ever be apprehended. The special agent expected no ransom. He feared that even as he conducted his interrogation the stolen child was being spirited farther and farther away from the scene of the crime, perhaps into white slavery in a backward nation.

In fact, Bernard, about-to-be Scooter, was still quite close by. After leaving Los Angeles, Roman Loon had driven through the blowing night straight up the Ventura freeway to his home in Santa Barbara. Throughout the drive Roman hummed and giggled, and Scooter sniffled and snored.

Santa Barbara is unique and blessed among the major towns on the Southern California coast in that it lies at the confluence of peak and brine. Natives have dotted the foothills that loom above their town with adobe houses and red-tiled roofs. These scenic hillsides have been dubbed "the Riviera."

Marian Loon lived with her husband in a small apartment on this Riviera. The Loon neighbors were mostly carpenters, retired business people, and writers. When Roman pulled his VW microbus into the much-patched driveway, it was still dark. There was, however, a candle burning in the window, barely visible through a stand of eucalyptus. Marian, caught up a bit in Roman's fascination with Britannia, kept the small flame burning for her husband whenever he was out on what he referred to as "a mission."

At the sound of her husband's motor Marian leapt up from her favorite reclining chair and was at the door even as Roman lifted sleeping Scooter out of the front seat.

"Hi-hi-hi," said Marian Loon, rushing to unflap the pack.

"Mission successful," said the cat burglar.

"My God, I think he's dead," said Marian, staring down at the motionless child.

"He's just asleep," replied Roman, gathering his gear. "Infants do that, you know."

"I have a bottle ready," said Marian, holding Scooter awkwardly until Roman was ready to go into the house. "Do you think he's hungry?"

"A moment ago you thought he was dead, now you want to know if he's hungry. Give him a little time, he'll let us know."

"Waaahaaaiiiii," said Scooter.

Marian grinned the biggest grin Roman Loon had ever seen in his life.

"He's letting us know," she said.

3

The hunt for the mistoed Bernard Steinberg did not come to a discreet end. Instead, it just faded away. Investigations that have little chance for success require constant threats and badgering by the concerned party to maintain forward motion, and Adam did not push. Initially, Sharon Steinberg was as wounded and mortified as any bereaved mother, and she urged Adam to keep hounding the police.

"Go to the press," she told her husband. "Just have them spread a description of Bernard all over the country."

At the outset Adam had no interest whatsoever in recovering his malformed infant son. He could not share his secret relief with his grieving wife, so he refused to pressure anyone on the grounds that the child was probably already across the border into Canada or Mexico and that the authorities were therefore powerless. He also pointed out that it would do his practice and her social standing little good to be needlessly portrayed as pathetic victims.

Without lawyer Adam's political clout, the pursuit of Bernard was shelved in favor of more pressing matters. As the kidnapping receded in everyone's memory, the Bel Air lawyer began to wrestle with his own guilt. He woke sweating in the night, little toes and fingers dancing before his bleary eyes.

"Take it as a sign," his Yale gynecologist buddy advised.

"Since when are you superstitious?" asked Adam. "You're a man of science. You don't believe in all that hoopla."

"Hoopla?" said the doctor.

"You know, omens, signs, the occult, that sort of thing."

"I'm not claiming anything of the sort," said the doctor, who was interested only in staying out of jail so he could continue to poke the ravishing wife of the baby-gang leader. "I'm simply saying that maybe this is all for the best."

"What do you think has happened to him?" asked Adam.

"I'm sure he is very happy, wherever he is," said the doctor. "I'm sure he is well clothed, warm, and well fed, cherished by people who can have a baby no other way."

"I have these terrible dreams," said Adam.

"Perfectly natural," the doctor soothed. "They will fade with time."

"And Sharon. She's inconsolable. She weeps, she can't hold a conversation, she clutches the pictures I took in the hospital before I, ah, noticed."

"I suggest you get started making another baby as soon as you can."

"I said the same thing to her," said Adam. "Do you know what she said to me?"

"I can't guess," said the doctor, wearying quickly.

"She said that I should have some respect. She said that Bernard was not a pet gerbil to be mourned briefly and then replaced."

"Of course," said the doctor. "Those feelings, too, will fade."

On the surface the tragic case of Bernard Steinberg continued to be pursued by the Federal Bureau of Investigation, but in fact Scooter was added to a long list of ongoing and unsolved cases. Adam Steinberg took his old pal's advice and turned his romantic steam on Sharon. Adam knew how to play the game, even with his wire-rimmed glasses on, and he dearly loved both his wife and the order in his world. Lawyer Adam so badly wanted things to return to their former certain way that he strove tirelessly to erase the memory of the gerbil Bernard from his wife's mind. Sharon had her own cherished dreams of home and hearth, and she gradually responded, opening her heart to her husband once more.

Ironically it was Adam who could not finally succeed in erasing the memory of his son, probably because he still felt guilty about not doing more to get him back. With the help of his male hormones, he set to work trying to produce a new boy, and his feelings became like a gnarled bonsai tree, twisting and rooting inside him and forever being trimmed back.

If Sharon and Adam could have wished upon Scooter a foster father of higher moral fiber than Roman Loon, they could not have wanted for him a finer boyhood town than Santa Barbara. As the thin FBI file on Scooter became dustier and dustier, Scooter Loon became a bike-and-canyon toddler.

A short ways east of the house of Loon, a road stretched north and south along the edge of the Riviera, meeting in its course the twisting scenic highway through San Marcos Pass. It was up this road, with a view west to the Mediterranean rooftops of Santa Barbara and a view east to the Santa Ynez Valley, that Roman Loon took Scooter to learn to climb and shoot. While not a violent man at heart, Roman felt that it was part of his great cat-burgling heritage to be proficient in the traditional tools of his trade. He scorned automatic weapons in favor of traditional revolvers, those with long, snouting barrels that could hold and coddle a bullet straight to its target from afar. With Scooter strapped swaddled to his belly and a knapsack full of handguns on his back, Roman Loon pierced the mountains on his BSA motorbike.

Usually the morning air was so cold that little Scooter shivered as he clung and stared ahead, sandwiched between his dad's chest and the cold British metal of the BSA's gas tank. Because these early rides were repeated so many times during the first five years of his life, they became an integral and indelible part of Scooter's past. It was his eagerness for these hair-raising jaunts that provided Roman Loon with his new son's name.

"We have to call him something," said Marian at the celebration of Scooter's first birthday. Neither of the Loons knew what Scooter's real date of birth was, but they arbitrarily determined that he had entered their lives at one week of age. Marian Loon made this determination by avidly reading every baby book she could find, and she assessed Scooter's development with astonishing accuracy. Although nobody knew it, she had Scooter pegged to the day.

"How can we name him when we don't know what he's like?" countered Roman.

"People always name their kids before they know what they're like," said Marian. She even started to point out that Scooter had a name before they got him, but she stopped herself before the words were formed because she knew that Roman would not tolerate any reference to Scooter's past. By mutual accord, that subject was taboo.

"Just because people always do it doesn't mean we have to," said Roman. "It just doesn't make any sense."

"Well, what am I going to call him when he scoots around?" asked Marian. "I can't just yell 'hey you' or go 'tssss' like you do to a dog."

"Who else would we be speaking to when we call him?" asked her husband. "There's just you and me and him."

The Loons had few friends, and Scooter's existence was as closely held a secret as Roman's lechery. The fact that they kept Scooter as secret as they did was a testimonial not only to the boy's quiet disposition but to the extraordinary attention to detail that attends the mind of the cat burglar. Roman tied Scooter's offal in opaque plastic bags that muffled both the sickly sweet baby smell and the sight of the contents within. He paneled Scooter's nursery in soundproof materials so that even the occasional wail passed without revealing the child even to the sparrows outside.

Scooter's health, if not his form, was as robust as any parent could pray for. Despite clandestine early morning motorbike rides, and long hours climbing through dust and glass and cricket wings, Scooter was as strong as an iron casing. Since he never got sick, Marian could not protest his participation in burglar-training activities.

Roman favored a .22 caliber revolver made for the matches at Bisley, England. The barrel was nearly nine inches long, and the handle was mother-of-pearl. The trigger pull was set at two and a half pounds, and Scooter, with his extraordinary hands, and with his father's guidance, could manage to send off a round or two. On his second birthday Roman dressed the boy in new corduroy overalls, stuffed his ears with cotton at the insistence of his mother, and took him up through San Marcos Pass on the 1968 BSA Rocket Three for a bottle-breaking spree.

"We're going to hike up those rocks," said Roman, pointing to some boulders off the road. "And then we're going to have some fun."

The first shot that Scooter managed, sitting amid the rocks and shed pieces of rattlesnake skin, took the top off of a bottle of Moët and Chandon champagne, sending the white foam groundward. Roman leapt up, retrieved the bottle from where it stood, and brought it back to the boy. Parting his lips with an area of smooth glass, Roman gave Scooter his first drink. They spent the rest of the afternoon shooting and drinking, until Roman stretched out to sleep in the late summer sun and misfingered Scooter, born Bernard, curled up beside him. When they finally rode home Roman Loon was sober and Scooter wasn't even cold.

"Hike," said Scooter, as he walked through the door of the Loons' Riviera apartment.

"Did you hear that?" cried Marian. "He talked."

"Hike-hike-hike," said Scooter Loon.

"He's talking about my scooter," said Roman with a grin. "I knew he loved to ride."

"He didn't say 'bike,' " said Marian, "he said 'hike.' "

Roman Loon had developed keen senses for his work atop roofs and balustrades. His hearing, however, was no longer acute, having been in steady decline since his early years shotgunning ducks.

"Bike," the crook insisted.

"Hike," said his wife. "Just listen."

"Bike," said Roman. "I know motorcycle talk when I hear it." Roman shook his head proudly. "He's in love with two-wheelers, just like his old man. Two years old and he just loves to scoot around."

"He's saying 'hike,' " said Marian Loon.

"I've got it," said her husband.

"Thank God."

"I've got a name for him," said Roman Loon.

4

Marian Loon was a self-edu-
cated woman. This meant that she had read and read and
read, forming hypotheses and testing them with a true and
natural scientific mind. Though logical and well informed,
Marian's studies went unguided and were constantly at the
mercy of her ignorant and dogmatic husband. Though she
would admit to no prejudice against a life of snaking about
rooftops in order to steal from people, Marian was adamant
that her son not follow, literally, in his father's footsteps.

Scooter's education presented major problems for Marian
and Roman Loon. They were anxious that Scooter flourish
and develop, but afraid to admit to the world that he was
theirs for fear of having to explain Marian's invisible pregnancy. The first four years of Scooter's life were thus spent in
the bosom of the Loons' Riviera apartment, playing in the
yard with Roman's pit bull and slumbering in a soundproofed
nursery. Roman had predictably named the dog Stud and had
fenced in the yard with high dark planks that, to his landlord's
delight, he paid for himself.

Roman's contribution to Scooter's early education was to
show him books filled with old black-and-white photos of
prowlers on London ledges with great billows of industrial
effluvia in the background. Beyond books, of course, were the
motorcycle rides into the canyons to shoot guns and drink
booze.

Marian had a more broad-minded and traditional view. She
read that infants need stimulation to develop active minds, so
she suspended stimulating items from clothespins and coat
hangers. Paper dragons, big and yellow inflatable dinosaurs
with glaring eyes and sketched-in teeth hung above the junior

Loon's crib. Some time later Marian added graph paper covered with trigonometric expressions and half-erased lines found in the trash at the public library. Never wanting to be left out of Scooter's life, his father contributed bullet casings, killed and dried potato bugs, and busted bits of motorcycle to the educational mobile.

"What's this bug going to teach him?" demanded Marian. "He's going to have nightmares about those pinchers."

"Pincers, not pinchers," said Roman. "You put up great-toothed dinosaurs with terrible eyes and you tell me he's going to have bad dreams about a potato bug?"

"The dinosaurs are blowups," said Marian. "The bug is real."

"He doesn't know that," said Roman.

"He doesn't know the bug is dried up either," said Marian. She wanted to rip the stiff insect off the line and throw it away, but she was afraid to touch it.

"Trigonometry," said Scooter, tapping the pyramids on paper until they swung back and forth.

Both his parents stared at him in stunned silence.

"Hoo," said Roman.

"And you say he doesn't know the dinosaur balloons aren't real," said Marian.

Marian had read enough Dr. Spock books to know that she had lucked into an exceptional child, more exceptional than she could probably have produced from her own loins.

"I think it's unusual for a child to recognize trigonometry when he's less than three years old," said Marian, trying to be matter-of-fact.

"Successful surgeon," said Scooter Loon.

"I understand the trigonometry," said Roman slowly, staring at the revolving piece of discarded graph paper, "but where did he get the surgeon stuff?"

"I said something yesterday," said Marian Loon.

"What did you say?"

"I told him that if he was a good boy and tried to understand all the things I taught him, that he'd grow up to be a successful surgeon."

"You think he knows what that means?" Roman scoffed.

"I know he's no parrot, if that's what you're getting at."

"He listens to you, he listens to the TV."

"I've never said the word *trigonometry*."

"Well, I know he didn't hear it from me," said Roman Loon.

The trigonometry incident triggered some kind of acceleration in Scooter's development. It was as if he had been biding his time, quietly listening and watching, and suddenly decided it was time to let on. By the time Scooter Loon was four he had learned everything that his mother could teach him. He argued with her that Pluto was not the planet farthest from the sun. That honor, he explained patiently, went to Neptune, whose elliptical orbit put it beyond Pluto at the apogee of its travels. Scooter devoured books, television programs, magazines, and chemistry sets so voraciously that, in quiet moments alone, Marian sometimes had the sense that she might be cooking for some alien creature that was going to grow to be the size of a house.

Scooter was also one of the fortunate and rare children whose physical attributes matched his mind. True, he had an odd number of fingers and toes, but he also had his natural mother's thick auburn hair. He had Adam Steinberg's piercing blue eyes and was of sound and medium frame, well coordinated and energetic. Roman Loon loved to play with the boy, but for a time found him to be distant and self-preoccupied. The interval between Scooter's fourth and sixth birthdays were years of deep depression for Roman, who felt that some great and cruel joke had been played, resulting in him having a son who no longer showed any interest in guns and motorcycles and never had shown any in burgling.

As he grew, Scooter Loon played more and more roughly with Stud, until one afternoon, when the sun was very, very bright and the wind was blowing hot and dry as it had the day he was stolen, Scooter pushed the pit bull too far. The boy had just turned five, and he was anxious to show Stud that he was no longer an infant, no longer a babe to be gently guarded, watched out for, drooled upon. He grabbed the dog's pendulous testicles in his hand and yanked. Being of unsound breeding, as are many a backyard cross between the English and the Staffordshire bull terrier, Stud let out a yelp, folded sideways like a pretzel, and took Scooter's head in his jaws.

The dog's teeth punctured the skin above Scooter's ears, leaving a scar he would always bear as a reminder that there is a limit to things, even if you are five years old and believe the world goes on forever. Scooter's screams brought Roman running. The cat burglar emerged into the white light with his favorite pearl-handled revolver in his hand. Marian Loon followed close behind.

If there was ever a moment in her short life when she wondered whether her husband loved her son, it was the moment Marian saw Roman hesitate in the backyard. Scooter fell strangely silent as he looked up from the ground at his father. Their eyes locked until the blood rushing over Scooter's brow made him blink.

Marian completely misunderstood her husband's lack of action. The problem was not that Roman didn't love his son—the problem was how much he loved his dog. The cur had the sort of go-to-hell-if-you-don't-like-me attitude that Roman cultivated in himself. Roman tolerated it when Scooter played with the dog because he knew it was ridiculous to be possessive in the face of a little boy's desire for communion with an animal. There had been times, however, when he had watched the way Scooter stroked the dog and felt, like we all do about our pets and loved ones, that his own strokes were really the only right ones and that the dog could not possibly enjoy another's touch.

Roman may have been frozen with emotion, but Marian was not. Although she had always adamantly refused to learn to shoot, she grabbed the revolver out of her husband's hands and crossed the yard in two steps. An utterly flat expression on her face, she put the revolver to the dog's head and pulled the trigger.

Marian's hand was shaking so badly that the bullet did not fly true but merely grazed a furrow in Stud's flesh, at the part of the animal's muzzle called the stop. The hound's eyes rolled back into his head and he let Scooter go. Then he went panting and howling across the yard to take refuge in the little dog-house with a red-tile roof that Roman had built for him to match all the other Riviera homes.

Abruptly the thief broke into action, scooping his son up in his arms and holding his face so close that the blood smeared both of them. Scooter's whole body was shaking, and he clutched his father tightly. Marian, the gun still warm at her side, closed in like a homing raptor and folded her arms around them both. When the shaking stopped Roman had a look at Scooter's wounds. As he ran his thumb gently over the holes, Scooter looked into the cat burglar's eyes.

"You saved me," he said.

"It wasn't me," said Roman. "Your mother shot the dog."

"But you wanted to."

"I wanted to," said Roman.

"You just love Stud too," said Scooter.

Marian began to cry.

"Stud's okay," she said.

5

When Scooter Loon was about to have his fourth birthday, Sharon Steinberg gave birth to her second child. She had refused the tests that reveal birth defects in utero, arguing with Adam and her scheming doctor that such tests would "jinx" the baby. Her real reason for refusing the tests was that she was determined to have the child even if it came out looking like a lizard. The prospect of losing another infant, even a nameless, formless one, was more than she could bear.

The child emerged without any aid from the doctors or nurse-midwives. Sharon was so afraid that something would go awry and the baby would be grabbed from her and drowned in a bucket of disinfectant that she endured labor with barely a moan, her wet face swollen and red, her teeth gritted from the effort. Only after she had pulled the child to her and seen that it was intact did she ring for the nurse.

Since Adam had not arrived by the time the papers had to be filled out, it was up to Sharon to choose the baby's name herself. The Steinbergs had not discussed the possibility that the child would be a girl. Big on dreams, Adam had awakened in a glorious trance about halfway through Sharon's term to announce that he had seen the child and it was another boy. Sharon doubted the dream and was almost glad it had been baseless.

"We were told it would be a boy," Sharon lied to the nurse.

"Who told you?"

"The men that gave me that test."

"Odd," said the nurse. "Well, anyway, you have given birth to a beautiful baby girl."

"I know that," said Sharon. "I've got eyes."

"We must have a name for the record."

"But I don't have a name."

"We can't leave it blank," said the nurse. "Just give me something, anything. You can always change it later."

"Gigi," said Sharon suddenly. "Like the movie."

A name is a peculiar thing. It takes time to settle in, to develop a relationship with its person. If changed too quickly or too often, a name is wont to take something away with it, forever diminishing its namesake or leaving behind a mercurial spark. The wet nurse had observed that new mothers are as likely to change their minds as people who have just acquired a puppy, and she did not want the little Steinberg girl to be dissipated in any way by the application of an impromptu choice. Ironically, in her haste, she caused the precise condition she was so anxious to avoid.

"Biji it is," she said, scribbling quickly and dashing from the room before Sharon could correct her.

Sharon rolled the name around on her tongue a bit, then chucked her new baby under the chin. "Biji," said Sharon.

When Adam arrived he tried to hide his dismay. He realized that he was acting spoiled because things had not come out precisely his way. He covered his mixed feelings with an outrageous overplay of affection.

"She's so cute, she's so cute, she's so cute," he cooed. We have to think of a name." He cradled the white blanket that held the child next to his face so that his whiskers turned the baby's face red.

"I have one already," said Sharon.

"You've named her for your mother," said Adam.

"Wrong," said Sharon with a smile.

"From your smile I can see that you've named her for *my* mother."

"Wrong again," said Sharon.

"You've named her for a famous film star."

"Wrong," said Sharon.

"Listen to her," said Adam. "Hear those noises she makes? Let's call her Greta Garble."

"Not Greta," said Sharon. "Biji."

Sharon's initial evaluation notwithstanding, Biji was defective. While her brother's malformation could be passed off as subtle but unattractive, Biji featured an anomaly that would only enhance her beautiful features and lush figure when she became a full-grown woman. Biji's right eye was deep green and her left was pale blue.

While Biji and Bernard shared the grand majority of their genetic material, their environment was as different as if one had been born in Papua New Guinea and the other had been born to seal-hunting Eskimos. While Bernard was being tutored at home by Marian Loon, Biji was being driven about in Sharon Steinberg's convertible Mercedes. In the morning Sharon took her little girl to private school, and in the afternoon to tennis lessons. While Scooter was busting through the canyons on the front of Roman Loon's BSA motorbike, Biji was sitting next to her mother at a children's performance of Tchaikovsky's *Nutcracker Suite.*

Whatever magic there was in the confluence of Steinberg sperm and seed had blessed Biji with all the phenomenal mental abilities of her lost brother. Biji's first word was *thesaurus.*

The Steinbergs recognized early on that they had a special baby. Sharon felt that this was only their due, that it was only right for Adam and her to have a child that was worth two, since they were missing one. Adam's reaction was somewhat different. Although he never said a word about it to Sharon, he wondered if perhaps his firstborn son was not alive somewhere, a genius doing credit to a false father.

6

Roman and Marian Loon knew instinctively that word of mouth was magically faster than sound itself, and the shooting of Stud provided a perfect opportunity to introduce Scooter to the community. The Loon household was flanked by two other Riviera dwellings. One house was close by and belonged to a deaf and retired gardener who would have failed to notice the nearby detonation of an atomic bomb. The other house was separated from the Loons' by a stand of eucalyptus and belonged to a housepainter and his wife. The Loons had been quite friendly with the painter before the advent of Scooter; Roman had even done some work with Mr. Whitbrush on a Santa Barbara estate that he subsequently robbed. Roman liked to joke that the man's name had led to his profession.

When Scooter arrived the Loons stopped seeing the Whitbrushes because of Norma Whitbrush's mouth. Norma noticed everything, from extra-white garbage bags filled with something to the increased frequency of Marian's trips to the grocery store, and she gossiped about everything. When Scooter began to play in the yard, which Roman had so thoroughly fenced in, Norma began to hear faint noises through the trees. When Marian shot the dog there was no keeping Norma out.

The doorbell rang a few moments after the shot was fired. Marian panicked, but Roman was used to moments of peril. Roman Loon could think on his feet.

"It's Norma Whitbrush," said Marian, peering through the peephole in the front door.

"Take Scooter to his room and wipe his face," said Roman, his hand still on the little boy's head. "When I've spoken to her for a few minutes, bring him out as if nothing's wrong."

When Marian opened the door Norma nearly fell in. Her ear had been pressed to the wood.

"I heard a shot," she said.

"A shot?" said Marian.

"I heard a gunshot. Is everybody okay?"

Marian invited Norma in, and when they were sitting together in the living room, reached forward and took her hands.

"Norma, I've got the most exciting news," whispered Marian.

Norma's eyes lit up.

"We've adopted a little boy."

"A little boy?"

"A child, we've adopted a child."

Norma Whitbrush looked like she wouldn't be able to stay in her chair. The day was turning into a gossip's dream.

At that moment Roman came out, leading Scooter by the deformed hand. Scooter was shy, since he almost never met people, but he managed to smile at Norma. Marian and Roman smiled at each other, because they knew that in that moment, when Norma Whitbrush grinned back at their little boy, Scooter Loon had become legitimate.

Unlike the student who excels only in topics he finds interesting, Scooter, once enrolled in a local Santa Barbara grade school, flourished like a desert flower in a flash flood. His academic successes came not from some astounding reservoir of self-discipline, but rather from the fact that all fields of study came to him so easily. His parents rarely saw him doing homework, yet he consistently brought home top grades.

Marian Loon made an active effort to stay abreast of Scooter's school topics. The former Steinberg was patient and loving with her, and read to her from his own essays and stories as well as discussing other topics with her. Mother and son spent countless hours together reviewing the fundamentals of algebra and reading Shakespeare to each other. It became standard practice for Scooter to buy two copies of every play or piece of fiction assigned to him so that his mother could follow along.

"Cassius," read Scooter, standing in the middle of the living room with his six-fingered right hand on his breast, "be not deceived if I have veiled my look. I turn the trouble of my incontinence merely upon myself, vexed I am of late, with passions of some difference—"

"Countenance, count-en-ance, not incontinence," said Marian, reading along with him. "Countenance means face, incontinence means, you know . . ."

"No, I don't know. What does incontinence mean, Mother?"

"It means that you go too often."

"Go too often?"

"You know"—Marian rolled her eyes skyward—"like after you eat too many prunes?"

"Prunes?"

"Brutus is saying that he wears an unhappy expression because he is upset inside. . . ."

"You mean he's sick about something?"

"Worrying, he's worried about something."

"OOOH," Scooter said slyly. "Brutus is worried because he has the craps!"

"You're doing this on purpose," said Marian Loon, throwing the book at her son with a great show of being mad.

Though he adored Roman, Scooter could not play with him this way. The cat burglar wanted nothing to do with Scooter's schoolwork, showing interest only at report time, when he rewarded his son's outstanding performance with a few dollars for a movie. It wasn't that Roman was uncaring or intransigent, but rather that he felt genuinely uncomfortable with Scooter's academic successes. Roman was a high school dropout who would sooner spit teeth than read Shakespeare.

Because Roman simply could not, it was up to Scooter to mend the growing rift. True to form, the boy tackled the problem with his rapacious appetite for facts and figures and his faultless memory. When Scooter was twelve his father went on a grand mission, a five-day span of derring-do that involved flint men, torches, shadows, and jewels. Scooter had only the vaguest sense that something was afoot, and this from the tension and short temper of his mother. Half to soothe his active

mind in something and half to please Roman upon the thief's
return, the former Bernard Steinberg read every single tome in
his father's vast motorcycle library. Scooter pored over details
of Ariel Arrows and took in the curved chrome crankcase of
the G50 Matchless. He learned the powerband of the Black-
shadow Vincent and the trials of Honda's early road machines.
He read with the ever-growing raptness that little boys alone
can muster of the racetrack exploits of racer Mike "the Bike"
Hailwood at the Isle of Man. In school, with his father gone
and motorcycles on his mind, Scooter Loon paid scant attention to his classwork. Marian, submerged in her own world of
worry, failed even to notice that Scooter was preoccupied.

Although Santa Barbara is generally considered part of that
palm and bikini oasis known to California locals as "the southland," it is more precisely part of the central coast. Its weather
patterns show ties to both the breezes of the Baja Peninsula to
the south and the mist and bite of Morro Bay to the north.
Winters in Santa Barbara are sometimes cold and are nearly
always wet.

The drizzly night of Roman Loon's return from the big heist
found Marian nervous, the window candle flickering, and
Scooter pretending to be asleep. The boy had left the window
in his room, formerly his soundproofed nursery, open. The
smell of wet eucalyptus was upon the bedsheets, and the slam
of a car door roused young Loon like a gong.

Roman Loon entered the house, and Scooter did what he
had never done before. He crept to the door and watched his
parents. Marian stayed in her rocking chair while Roman took
the coiled rope from about his shoulder and laid it gently on
the floor. Next he unslung a soft black bag, and the former
Steinberg heard it clink as it fell. At this Marian rose, and
when his father had taken off his wet things and shaken his
thin blond head like a lion, she was in his arms. In the candle-
light Scooter could not tell if he carried her or if she drove
him, but they moved together as stilts into the bedroom, and
Scooter followed.

Watching through the crack in the door, Scooter saw his
mother raise her arms as if pleading and saw his father slide

her dress up high. Marian Loon's features were too intense to be pretty, but her body, at least to Scooter's prepubescent eyes, was breathtaking. His father cupped and nuzzled her breasts and then they were upon the bed, all heaving and throwing and thrusting. Scooter knew of such things from school, he had even kissed a girl once, although she had eaten an anchovy pizza right before and he didn't much enjoy the taste. It seemed to him in some dim recess of his memory that all such lip locks brought out the fish in people. It wasn't what he saw that affected Scooter, for the candle was in the other room and there was barely any moon. What made his hands drip and his breath catch was the smell, an odor that went straight to his primitive reptilian hindbrain, that part of all of us where the triggers and clues of what we need to know are stored. Scooter had never felt such feelings, even rushing through the canyons at speed on two wheels. He backed away quietly, nearly tripping over the coffee table, and once back in his bed, he wept and wept and did not know why.

In the morning Marian Loon had a giant new red ring.

"Too bad about the Rocket Three," said Scooter over cornflakes.

"Too bad? What do you mean by 'too bad'? Did something happen while I was gone?"

"No, no, I don't mean about *your* Rocket Three," the boy said, "I mean about the model in general. You know that Triumph made the same bike?"

"The Trident," said Roman Loon.

Marian looked up from stirring pancake batter.

"Exactly," continued Scooter. "Those models spelled the demise of the British bike industry because Honda came out with its 750 Four."

"Demise?" said Marian Loon, wiping batter off of her new stone.

"Is this some kind of a joke?" asked Roman Loon.

"Well, the Japanese bike was faster and cheaper. It was good for a hundred and twenty, even though it didn't handle as well as the BSA, and the brakes on the Honda were better too."

By this time Marian Loon was not moving at all, and Roman had to work to move the hardening gobs of cereal to the back of his mouth and down his throat.

"Where did you hear all this?" asked Roman.

"Am I wrong?" asked Scooter.

"No, no," said Roman, leaning back until his chair rocked on the back two legs. "It's perfectly true. The big Honda was a death blow to the British, but there were other things too. Suzuki came out with a big bike soon after, as did Kawasaki, and then the British mismanaged their works so badly and Norton Villiers and BSA/Triumph merged into NVT and—"

"What I want is a Ducati," announced Scooter, wiping his mouth.

"You want a Ducati?"

"Nice and simple, light and handles well, I want to really learn to ride."

"No motorcycle for you," said mother Marian.

"How can you refuse me with a name like the one you gave me?" pursued the boy, watching his father closely.

"I didn't—" began Marian Loon.

"The boy's right," said Roman Loon. "He's old enough to have a bike to play with, in the dirt anyway."

"Will you get one, too, so we can ride together?" asked Scooter-born-Bernard, abandoning his breakfast to hug his father's arm.

Indeed, Roman Loon bought them identical Husqvarna Enduro bikes, high-quality Swedish motorcycles that could conquer any terrain. With these machines loaded in the back of his turbocharged pickup truck, Roman and his son would make for Bakersfield and other desert points, often leaving before sunrise on the weekend to maximize their time on two wheels. Roman taught Scooter everything he knew about tearing down engines, negotiating berms and trenches, using bike weight and body English, and selecting the right combination of gear and throttle. The two had races after jumping cactus and blowing sagebrush and chased jackrabbits through impossible terrain. Every gap they jumped, it seemed to Scooter, brought father and son closer together.

7

No matter how much he worried, Adam Steinberg's guilt-fueled imagination was no match for the realities of actually raising a daughter. Early on, Biji showed herself to be able to pit mother and father against each other in the way that single children do best. She cried and wailed for sympathy, and instigated arguments between her parents that were always resolved in her favor. Even in Bel Air, Biji's whims and wishes became legend.

One night, when she was eight years old, she came into her parents' bedroom. Adam appeared to be asleep, his arm over his eyes.

"All the other girls at school have earrings," said Biji.

"I gave you earrings with pearls in them," said Sharon.

"They're not pierced. All the rest of the girls have pierced earrings."

"To wear pierced earrings, you have to have pierced ears," said Sharon.

"And they have diamonds. All I have is pearls."

"Pearls are good enough," said Sharon. "Maybe we can talk about something with diamonds for your birthday."

"With diamonds and pierced?" said Biji.

"You're not piercing your ears," said Adam Steinberg, his voice muffled by his shirt sleeve. "Little girls don't have pierced ears."

"My teacher said she had her ears pierced when she was born," said Biji.

"Well, your teacher didn't have me for a father, and I say no pierced ears."

"I don't want diamonds really," said Biji. "Everyone has

diamonds. I want an emerald on one side and a sapphire on the other, to match my eyes. Nobody else has eyes like me."

"No pierced ears," said Adam, his arm still across his face.

"You can't get quality stones in clamp earrings," said Sharon. "Those earrings fall off too easily."

"See?" said Biji.

"Sounds like you're out of luck," said Adam.

Biji picked a pillow from the floor near her mother's side of the bed and hurled it at her father. Adam sat up with a start, his fingers flying to his crusty eyes, but Biji had already fled the room.

The next morning, while Adam was eating his breakfast, he heard Sharon scream. He dropped his toast on his tie and ran up the stairs to find her. She was in Biji's bathroom, clutching the little girl's head. There was blood everywhere.

"Oh my God," said Adam.

"She pierced her own ears with a pin," screamed Sharon. "Call the doctor."

Adam forced his wife's hands from Biji's head and looked at his daughter's ears. They were swollen and puffy, but the holes were clear.

"If I don't get some earrings," said Biji, locking eyes with her father, "I'm going to have to wear safety pins to school."

The fifteen years after Scooter's kidnapping saw a remarkable rise in the activities of the baby gang. The leader, cuckolded husband of the nurse assistant to Sharon Steinberg's gynecologist, grew bolder with each success. He continued to rob Mexican and poor white children from their cradles and homes and expanded his activities north and east as well, making off more frequently with the offspring of affluent folk. When Scooter was nearing his eighteenth birthday, and Biji Steinberg was just fourteen, the baby gang kidnapped the child of a major functionary of the San Francisco consulate of the nation of Japan. The infant's mother was strolling the heavily touristed halls of the city's Japan Center at the time, pushing the child in a pram, English style.

The baby thieves made a terrible ruckus, the design being to hide the true purpose of their activities. They stole a Hitachi portable television for cover, dragged painted dragon flags from umbrella stands, and ripped pornographic magazines from the tight hands of shy Asian men, spreading chalk-white breasts and straight trim mounds through the shoppers. The Japanese consul's wife was overwhelmed by the melee and lost hold of her carriage. She saw it being spirited away not by anyone in particular that she could identify later, but rather by a tide of shouting hooligans responsible for a tremendous fuss.

The leader of the baby gang had nothing against Orientals. He had picked his target as a result of a newspaper article describing the newly appointed consul and his family. He hoped in his hardened heart that the missing baby would gain him a place in the papers. There was a quality of self-sabotage to his efforts, for he was getting tired of his successes at the game and bored with all the easy money. The personal challenge was no longer there, his home life was failing, and he was no longer hungry.

The baby-gang leader's efforts to attract law-enforcement attention were successful. Most intrigued and committed to bringing him to justice was the section head of the FBI's San Francisco office, the same special agent who had cut his teeth on another notorious series of childnappings some eighteen years earlier in Los Angeles. The special agent had nothing to link the crimes except his personal frustration at failing to bring the criminals to justice. The modus operandi of the two incidents could not have been more different, not only because one was committed in the street and the other covertly in a home, but because one was executed with the stealth and near perfection that characterized the work of Roman Loon, while the other was carried out by far lesser men.

Niles Grosbeak's ire erupted, and he began to tighten the noose around the baby gang. He nosed and rooted for evidence and connections, and methodically he unearthed them. Little by little the gang members discovered themselves ostracized from both the criminal community and the baby brokers as whispered word of the G-man's interest spread. The baby-gang

leader, on the one hand getting what he had been asking for
and on the other shocked by the looming possibility of prison,
began to frazzle and fray. His arctic relationship with his phi-
landering wife, Clea, deteriorated to outright hostility and
then divorce. All operations halted for a time as the gang at-
tempted to cover their tracks and lay low.

No longer attached, the gynecologist's assistant turned her
attentions anew on Adam Steinberg's Yale buddy. Over the
years the buxom frigid nurse had kept the doctor's fires alight
by giving him just enough nooky but never too much, giving
him just enough attention but not always when he wanted it.
Clea worked hard at aerobics and dance and became more and
more attractive, as lucky women do, as she reached her late
thirties. Cold and scheming people are often able to see things
that the rest of us will not, and Clea played the doctor's heart
strings like the mistress of a very rich and twisted marionette.
Within two months of her divorce she wore the doctor's plati-
num engagement ring and drove his Maserati convertible
while he used her Jeep. Their relationship no longer a secret,
the pair began to socialize together, and before too long were
invited to the warm and happy home of Sharon, Adam, and
Biji Steinberg.

At eighteen years old, Scooter
Loon's sister was four years deflowered. She already showed
more than hints of a mature shape, being tall and slightly
olive-skinned, with lithesome proportions that would later
guarantee her the front pages of fashion and theater tabloids.
Biji seemed to have utterly bypassed that gangling, bone-set-
ting period that one sees in young victims of puberty's wiles.

"You're very lovely," said Clea, taking Biji's warm tanned
hand in her white cold one and staring at her eyes.

"You're probably wondering why I don't wear colored contacts," Biji replied, taking an instant dislike to this woman
whose bosom was so big and her mouth so small.

Clea turned red and dropped Biji's hand.

"Biji," said Sharon.

"I think your eyes are wonderful," the doctor said quickly. "They are such an unusual trait, and from what I hear from your father and mother, you are a very unusual girl."

"Weren't you married before?" Biji said to Clea.

"Pwooouugh," said Adam Steinberg, spitting a peanut across the room. Everyone except Biji pretended not to notice.

"Gross," said the little Steinberg.

Adam took his daughter by the shoulder and guided her away from the company and in toward the kitchen, where the cook was making a Cajun jambalaya with too much red pepper just for spite.

Biji was as precocious as her older brother, and every bit as talented in school. Though she was not an evil person, she was quite taken with herself, and not nearly as popular as Scooter. Biji's interest lay in the theater, and her elegant features and perfect skin landed her parts aplenty. And she had talent. The youngest Steinberg could shed and don hostility or warmth as easily as a T-shirt fresh from the dryer. Perhaps less than ingenuous in her personal relations, Biji was born to the stage and she knew it.

"Are you making the stew too hot again?" Biji asked her mother's cook. The cook, a slight, dark-skinned Jamaican woman who loved Biji as a sister, grinned, showing very white teeth.

"And how did you know that, Miss Biji?"

"You get this look on your face when you stir," said Biji. "It tells me you're mad about something. What happened, did you miss a date with your boyfriend tonight?"

"And last Tuesday, too, when your mother suddenly wanted high-fashion ladies to dinner."

"Well, that makes two of us," Biji sighed. "I was up for some Hollywood action tonight myself, if you know what I mean, but my dad wanted the doctor to see me for some reason."

"You sick?" the cook demanded in mid-stir.

"That's just the point. There's nothing wrong with me at all."

"You pregnant, Miss Biji?"

"He's not going to give me an exam between the pâté and the stew, now is he?"

"Where I come from doctors can plain smell you out. A woman's smell changes, you know, when she's with child."

"Are you a midwife now too?" asked Biji, staring intently at the stew and then sticking her finger and licking the red off.

"Shrimps in there," said the cook gravely.

"Could you smell if I was pregnant?"

"I'm no doctor," said the cook, "but I know what I know."

8

The cat-burgling profession, if it can be called that without tongue in cheek, inflicts upon its practitioners the same hardships as does any free-lance vocation. The cat burglar, just like the practicing psychologist, advertising consultant, or yacht skipper, must generate his own business as well as exercise his craft. He must, in short, create his own market and then take advantage of it.

In his time Roman Loon had heisted enough objets d'art, gold, and precious gems to fill a small auction hall. He fenced the stolen goods carefully, lived frugally with Marian, and invested wisely. He had experienced close scrapes with the law, but had never been convicted and imprisoned, and he knew enough to count himself lucky. Roman had a fine sense of when to quit, and as Scooter's last year of high school drew to a close, the second-story man did a stupendous thing. He made the move to legitimate business and opened a small shop dedicated to the sale and service of classic and exotic motorcycles.

"I think it's an absolutely incredible idea," said Marian Loon.

"Great idea, Dad," said Scooter.

"What are you going to call the shop?" asked Marian.

"I have a name," said Roman slyly.

"Give," said Scooter.

"I want to run it by you both. I don't want you to think I've already had the sign painted or anything."

"Give," said Scooter again.

"If you two don't like it, I won't use it. We can think of another name."

"Goddamnit, Dad, what's the name?" Scooter cried.

"Don't curse at your father," said Marian.

"Loon's Scooters," said Roman.

"Oh, Roman," said Marian.

"Kiss my ass," said Scooter.

In the end the mother and son settled on Loon Motors, and in the interests of domestic tranquillity, Roman acquiesced. The former burglar was hoping to interest Scooter in the shop, even though he knew that Scooter was destined for bigger things. Open and reasonable, for a thieving satyr, Roman offered his son a deal that was hard to refuse. If Scooter would work part-time to help build the business during his four undergraduate years, Roman would underwrite all of the young prodigy's tuition and living expenses.

What Roman did not know was that Scooter had been offered large and prestigious scholarships to schools across the nation. Yale, Adam Steinberg's alma mater, had offered to finance four years, and Harvard, Princeton, and Dartmouth had followed suit. The University of California was anxious to have Scooter in their computer department, and Scooter's astronomical test scores on college entrance exams had generated the best offer of all from Stanford.

Scooter's interest in motorcycles, which had seemed keen when he was a toddler, had waned during his adolescent years. Yet the boy was bright enough to realize that the older and more educated he became, the less he had in common with his father. Throughout his childhood Scooter strived to make Roman believe that he loved bikes just so that they would have something to talk about.

As so often happened in the days before youngsters made their own career choices, what had begun falsely and with force became effortless and true. Scooter tried so hard to be interested in motorbikes, living the part every day for eighteen years, that in the end his fervor indeed matched the older man's. Neither father nor son spoke of it, but the subtle yet significant shift took place during the first year of Loon Motors and was noticed by the whole family. In the end Scooter accepted both the Santa Barbara scholarship and Roman's offer, telling his father only that his tuition fees were quite low because he was taking few courses.

Roman deemed it only fitting that, as an advertisement for the shop, both he and Scooter should have the fastest, flashiest, classiest bikes in town, and that they should ride them everywhere. Roman's choice of play bike for himself told a great deal about the burglar's taste. It was a 1,000cc Laverda RGS in startling orange, with wheels and engine parts lovingly prepared by what had begun as an Italian tractor company. The curious thing about the Laverda was that, like Roman, it was a rebel, bucking every motorcycling trend in nearly every facet of its design. Roman loved it because it had three cylinders.

"That just doesn't seem sound," observed Scooter, helping his father break open the wooden box and uncrate the machine.

"Wait until you ride it," said Roman.

"But nobody makes a motorcycle with three cylinders. An odd number makes things rough, uneven. Two cylinders I can see, even though twins vibrate . . ."

Roman Loon lifted his eyebrows at this.

". . . and four cylinders makes a great deal of sense from the engineering standpoint, opposition of power pulses and all that. But a triple!"

"Just wait'll you ride it," said Roman Loon, who had made a thorough and lifelong study of motorcycle design and had found out that the Laverda was a marvel of sporting engineering.

While he loved to share in the older man's enthusiasm, Roman's unswerving tendency to choose the bizarre and different for the mere sake of it went against Scooter's cool and logical mind-set. After they had oiled the motor and adjusted the carburetors, Roman went around the block on the big machine and brought it back for Scooter to try.

"Look how the thing shakes," Scooter cried, lifting his leg over the hard black saddle.

"Wait'll you ride it," said Roman.

"You keep saying that," shouted Scooter over the staccato note of the exhaust. "But even if it rides well, it still shakes like an eggbeater and has three cylinders."

"Wait'll you ride it," Roman shouted back as Scooter took off in an easy racer's crouch.

Street motorcyclists are without question a breed apart. It takes a certain type of person to be willing to expose himself to the perils of the road, whether it be the merciless rush of asphalt just inches from one's feet, the vagaries of wind currents from oncoming trucks, or the uncertainties of near-blind octogenarians bent on making that left turn. When Loon Motors opened, Scooter's street-riding experience was limited to short rides on his father's old BSA and equally short rides on the mass-produced Japanese bikes ridden by his friends.

Scooter gunned the Laverda toward the mountains, finding it cumbersome and awkward on the Santa Barbara streets. He made for familiar San Marcos Pass and the curves he had enjoyed as an infant strapped over his father's gas tank. The big bike felt much better at speed, and Scooter began to understand that clumsy and slow around town meant rock stable and responsive as road speed climbed toward three digits. The canyon walls blurred beside him, and clods of light brown dirt whizzed beneath his wheels. He felt his way through banked turns, his body bent in line with the machine, his knee hanging to the inside of the curves. At last he reached a long straightaway, a perfect opportunity to explore the limits of the machine.

Perhaps he was thinking of what he would say to Roman, or perhaps he was looking briefly down at the instrument cluster. Whichever it was, Scooter failed to notice the gray truck bumper that lay across the road. At the last moment it dawned on him that the bumper was not a shadow or a trick of the light, but a large piece of metal directly in his path. Scooter countersteered suddenly, as Roman had shown him to do years before in the desert when encountering a berm or boulder. The leading right edge of the front tire skimmed the edge of the bumper, sending the twisted truck piece spinning into the opposing lane and then onto the shoulder. Scooter did not even feel the bike flinch, but the sudden rush of adrenaline made him want to vomit. He slowed the bike to a crawl and pulled onto the shoulder. Very carefully, for he was shaking like an inchworm in a breeze, Scooter Loon lowered the polished chrome kickstand, got off the motorcycle, and sank to his knees.

It would be fair to say that until that moment Bernard Steinberg had never thought about death. Eighteen-year-old boys usually don't, and even a child with so dramatic and theatrical an infancy as Scooter Loon doesn't believe in his own mortality until he faces death in some terrible last instant. The sun was beginning to wane out over the Pacific, and Scooter crouched for a long time beside the motorcycle, listening to the pings and pops of cooling metal and smelling mountain plants. When his nausea had subsided and the quivering in his hands was gone, Scooter pushed the bike until it faced down the hill and rode it gingerly back to the shop, feeling as if his mouth was lined with gauze.

"I was worried you might have stolen my baby," said Roman Loon as his son pulled in the driveway.

"One hell of a motorcycle, Dad," said Scooter Loon.

"Told you," said Roman. "But I've got a surprise for you, since you were nice enough to help me get this one ready."

"I've had enough surprises for one day, okay, Dad? I have studying to do, a test in physical chemistry tomorrow and another one in Greek on Thursday."

"This surprise can't wait," said Roman with a wet, twinkling eye. Placing his hands on Scooter's shoulders, the wiry blond burglar pushed the boy back down onto the Laverda's seat.

"Just stay put for a moment," he ordered.

Scooter closed his eyes and slumped against the blue bike's smooth cowl.

"Keep those eyes closed," commanded Roman, amid creakings and clicks. "Now open them and feast on this."

Scooter opened his eyes and saw a bright red motorcycle, decidedly smaller than the one he still straddled. It was enclosed in swoopy bodywork, detailed in green and yellow, with stubby low handlebars clipped onto the front fork and less padding on the seat than might be afforded by a pair of Kleenex. Scooter looked at the 750 F1 Ducati, a machine that

he had admired with his father in pictures not three weeks
before. He looked up at Roman's proud tight face and noticed
several blond whiskers where the former criminal had forgotten to shave. The two locked eyes, and Roman gave his biggest, best smile. The moment his dad bent to the starter,
Scooter felt his eyes itch and fill.

"Wait'll you ride it," said Roman Loon.

"Dad," began Scooter, "I can't take it for a ride right now."

"Just wait'll you ride it," said Roman Loon as Scooter
swung a leg over.

9

Biji was not pregnant, as she teasingly led her mother's cook to believe, at least not that night of her fourteenth year when the doctor and Clea came to dinner. Her pregnancy did not come until four years later. She discovered it the day that Roman Loon opened the doors of Loon Motors for business. She had missed her monthly period for the second time, and having always been regular as the new moon, she became worried and purchased a home pregnancy test kit from the local drugstore. The solution turned the telltale color, and Biji went looking for someone in whom she could confide her ill fortune.

The natural thing would have been to discuss the matter with the father-to-be, but Biji had little idea who he was. Like many Beverly Hills teenagers with acting aspirations, and with plenty of her father's money, the youngest Steinberg enjoyed altering her consciousness and embracing life—and boys— with wild abandon. Biji was rapidly fulfilling the promise of her entrancing good looks and was always in demand. She had many acquaintances, almost as many lovers, and few friends. Like most beautiful women, she had trouble trusting anybody.

The pregnancy brought about a profound change of mood in Biji. She was always frank, even acerbic, but the ruthless pulse of hormones and her frustration in feeling she had no one to turn to made her withdrawn and hostile. One morning, when she failed to appear for breakfast, Sharon climbed the stairs to check on her.

"Time to wake up," said Sharon brightly, knocking on the door to Biji's room, the same room from which Roman Loon had stolen Bernard years before.

"Go away," mumbled Biji Steinberg into her pillow.

"Biji, honey, you're going to be late for school."

"I'm not going to school," said Biji.

"Are you sick?"

There was a pause, and then Biji coughed.

"Are you sick, honey?" Sharon asked again.

"No."

"Then why aren't you going to school? Will you unlock this door so I can talk to you? You know I hate it when you lock your door."

"You're talking now, aren't you?" said Biji.

"What if something were to happen? What if there were a fire in there from the electric blanket?" said Sharon. "What if there were a gas leak somehow and you were choking to death and we couldn't get in?"

"This isn't the kitchen and I don't have an electric blanket," said Biji.

"What if you slipped in the shower and bumped your head and got knocked out and the shower was running, or the bath, and you were drowning and making a flood?"

"I'm in bed," said Biji.

"I'm not talking about now, I'm just worried," Sharon said, rattling the door handle. "Now will you unlock the door?"

"What makes you think there's something wrong?" said Biji.

"I think there's something wrong because you are late for school and today is an important day."

"Really," said Biji in her best sarcastic tone.

"Your father has set up a screen test for you," said Sharon, rattling the handle again. There was a thump and the paddle of feet.

"He has?" said Biji, opening the door.

"My God, you look awful," said Sharon.

"That's nice."

"I know, I know, it's morning and you haven't gotten up. Still, you look terrible. You don't look well at all."

"I'm fine," said Biji.

The fact that Murray Feldman was short and dumpy just enhanced his image as a brilliant producer. What else but brains, people wondered, could have made him as successful as he was?

"Honestly, she's a knockout," Adam told Murray in a confident tone.

"You'll forgive me saying so," said the film man, "but every father thinks that about his daughter."

"Listen," said Adam impatiently, "this girl's really a knockout. She's going to make it, I know she is. She's talented."

Little fat Feldman rounded the desk and took the lawyer's hand as gently as if he were cupping a butterfly.

"Adam," he began, "you helped me with the studio contract, you helped me out of a sticky situation with my directors. I appreciate it and I am gonna do something for your kid. But I want you to understand something. There's a lotta girls out there, see? There's a lotta beautiful blondes with big blue eyes and gorgeous tits. And there's a lotta people pushing these girls, Adam, and that's just the way it is. If it were my kid, I wouldn't even let her get near this business. Tell her to marry a nice Jewish lawyer," rasped Murray, "and have a kid of her own."

"Biji's not blond," said Adam. "She's got red-brown hair and her eyes are green and blue."

"Biji?" said Murray Feldman the big-wheel producer. "You named your kid Biji?"

"I didn't pick the name. Sharon picked it."

"Sharon picked it," repeated Murray. "So your kid's name is . . ."

"Biji Steinberg," said Adam, feeling suddenly uncomfortable.

"A Jewish kid with mismatched eyes named Biji Steinberg." Murray chuckled in an unfriendly way. "I love it. You know that if we put her on film, she's gonna have to change her name."

"I don't see why," said Adam.

"I bet you don't, and that's why I'm the producer and you're not," said Murray Feldman.

Biji had a large bowl of cereal with strawberries that she took from a green plastic basket while Sharon hovered. After eating, and submitting to Sharon's cool palm on her head, Biji went to the garage and started her car.

While her parents had offered her a brand-new BMW, Biji had seen the car she wanted in a Burbank used-car lot. Sharon had complained bitterly that it was inappropriate and gas-guzzling, but Adam had secretly been pleased, knowing the car would cost considerably less than a new German sports model.

The car she chose was a barely used emerald-green 1967 rag-top Cadillac de Ville. The paint matched the hue of Biji's right eye, at least in the daylight, and watching from the portico it occurred to Sharon as Biji roared away that her daughter had been right about the big car. It dwarfed her, but still it suited her well.

Biji turned into a gas station on Wilshire Boulevard, pulled up to a pay phone, and looked up the number of her mother's gynecologist. She realized the risk she ran by contacting the family doctor, but she just couldn't think of anything else to do. The idea of going to a public clinic frightened and appalled her.

"This is Biji Steinberg," she said to the doctor when he came on the phone.

"How are you, Biji?" the gynecologist said. "What a nice surprise."

"I have to come see you right away," said Biji.

"Is it an emergency?"

"It's an emergency," said Biji, and hung up.

The gynecologist's office was in a long low building with sand-colored stones and deep brown windows. Since becoming the doctor's wife, Clea no longer worked in the office, spending her time instead shopping for diamonds to catch the light, cashmere sweaters too warm to wear, and shoes from Italy that pinched her broad feet. Biji didn't recognize the receptionist, but the elderly woman seemed to know her right away.

"You must be Biji Steinberg," said the woman, peering over wire-rimmed glasses that Biji thought were too small.

"Do I have to sit out here?" asked the girl.

The nurse seemed puzzled. "Is there something wrong?" she asked.

"I just don't want to sit out here with all these people," Biji hissed, close to the woman's ear.

"I see," said the nurse. "Well, perhaps you could sit on the chair in the X-ray room until the doctor is ready to see you."

"Yes," said Biji, taking a two-year-old *Vogue* magazine from the coffee table and avoiding the disapproving eyes of several forty-year-old women who sat with prim, crossed legs.

The X-ray room had a poster-sized painting of well-lit grapes and pears in a thick glass bowl. The picture covered a good portion of the wall above the leatherette couch. Biji sat on a small black stool that swiveled when she tapped her foot. If the bright fruit was meant to help her relax, it was a failure. She remained there for twenty minutes, holding and turning the pages of the magazine with her left hand while her right remained unconsciously spread between her legs.

"Biji," said the doctor, entering at last and startling her. "You are so mysterious. Is something the matter?"

"Of course," said Biji. "This isn't a social call."

The doctor exhaled. "Your parents don't work you much on manners, do they, Biji?"

"I'm pregnant."

"Ah."

"I want you to cut it out."

"You want an abortion?"

"I'm eighteen years old. Do you expect me to have a baby?"

"Perhaps you should have thought of that before you had sex. Did you use some form of birth control?"

"The rhythm method," Biji said defensively.

The doctor sighed.

"I don't need a lecture," said Biji.

"You probably do," said the doctor, "but I'm not the one to give it to you."

"I want the abortion right now," Biji said. "I have a screen test to go to this afternoon."

"You won't be going to any screen test after a procedure," the gynecologist replied, sitting on the edge of the X-ray couch, his feet perched on the small lip that was there to help old women get a leg up.

"Can't you give me something so I can go?"

"What I can do is to talk to your parents about this and then schedule your surgery for later in the week if that is what everybody wants."

"Forget that," said Biji. "I don't want my parents to know."

"Biji, you're underage. I have to tell you mother and dad."

"Then I'll go to a clinic," said Biji.

"I will have to tell your parents anyway."

Biji stood up. "If you do that," she issued in measured tones, letting the old magazine fall to the floor with a slap, "I will tell them that the baby is yours."

The doctor stood, too, until he towered over the little Steinberg. He looked into her eyes for a moment.

"You little bitch," he said. "I just bet you would."

"You just bet right."

"I can do it tomorrow. First thing in the morning. If I do it now, you'll never make your screen test."

"I'll see you at seven thirty," Biji said with a toss of her head.

"Don't eat anything beforehand," said the gynecologist.

"Why should I have toast and eggs," asked Biji, "when I can have you?"

"Eighteen years old," the elderly receptionist said, half to herself, as Biji left the office. "I shudder to think of her at thirty."

"I shudder to think of her tomorrow," said the doctor.

10

Motorcyclists the world over have made Sunday rides a tradition, and Roman Loon loved tradition. The jaunts he took, however, were not as casual as they appeared. They were in fact formal lessons in roadcraft that the veteran rider gave his son.

"Always be aware of the road surface," Roman told Scooter one day as the Laverda and the Ducati burbled by the side of the road. The former burglar walked out onto the tarmac, pointed his toe at an oily smear in the center of the road, and drew his boot across it as gracefully as any ballet dancer.

"This central oil stripe is on every road. It comes from leaking engine pans, hoses, transmissions, and differentials. Never ride in it."

"I don't always see that stripe," said Scooter.

"It doesn't matter. It's always there."

Roman explained to Scooter about powerbands, torque peaks, and lines through turns.

"A turn is a curve," he said, "but your motorcycle should go only in a straight line."

"I'm not sure I see what you mean," said Scooter, "and I want to be real clear on this so I don't go slamming into the side of a mountain."

"Do you do any drawing with a protractor in your physics classes at the university?" asked Roman.

"I haven't used a protractor since high school," Scooter replied, and immediately felt sorry.

"Well, you know that if you draw a half circle, or any other curve, there is always a straight line that connects the two end points."

"I can see that."

"Well, you can use your bike to trace something close to that straight line through every turn. You can straighten out the curve, especially on a machine like yours. Follow me."

Roman set a brisk pace through the canyons below Santa Barbara, aiming for the road that led to Lake Casitas, a man-made fishing and boating spot, and then on to Ojai, a hot-spring haven for the wealthy and a reputed spiritual center.

Roman's big Laverda was made for fast, gentle, sweeping turns and long straightaways. It gave up plenty to Scooter's Ducati when hustling down a twisty road as tight as the way to the lake. Roman was a veteran, though, and he muscled and leaned his machine into angles that brought flying sparks from the exhaust pipes and foot pegs, angles that made Scooter gasp into his helmet.

"I'm just afraid it will fall over," said Scooter when they pulled over. "I know it won't, I've seen you do it, I just have trouble with the fear."

"It's the gyroscopic effect of the wheels," Roman explained over the dull rumble of his triple, "that's what keeps the bike from toppling, especially when it's going more than about twenty miles per hour."

Scooter was secretly amazed to hear his father talk this way. Words such as *protractor* and *gyroscopic* were not normally part of Roman's vocabulary. What Scooter did not know was that the former burglar had spent hours boning up on the physics of motorcycling just so he would be able to impress his son with his erudition.

"Follow my lines through these turns now," said Roman. "I will take them slowly at first, and then once you've got the hang of them, we'll pick up the speed."

Scooter tapped the gearshift lever with the six toes that gave him so much trouble at the shoemaker. Extra-wide widths did not work, since his right foot was normal and went swimming in wide shoes. When he bought sneakers he cut a hole for the redundant toe. When he bought dress shoes they were spe-cially made. He had hammered and stretched his motorcycle boots so they caused him no pain. He nosed his Ducati out onto the tarmac, following the man who had stolen him from his crib. At first Roman's lines were deliberate and plodding. He used his bike as if it were a hand tracing the line onto the roadbed with deep blue ink. Gradually, with Scooter glued to his tail, he increased his speed until each curve was taken in a graceful turn.

Most people learn in a series of inclines and plateaus, and even with his formidable intellect, Scooter was no exception. Despite his occasional forays into the mountains and his early years swaddled warmly and hunched over the gas tank of his father's old BSA, Scooter had never really mastered the road. His riding had been competent but not relaxed, quick but not truly fast. This particular Sunday, however, his confidence increased by what his father had told him about the bike's stability, Scooter finally left the plateau on which his riding had rested for nearly a year.

Roman checked his mirror as often as his road speed would allow. He was surprised to see that Scooter did not drop back. The older man was seeking Scooter's limits so he could show his son exactly where his mistakes were.

The deep blue waters of Lake Casitas appeared to their right. The smell of sagebrush was heavy, almost as if it were an oil that clung to their jackets and tires. It is said that one's sense of smell is more closely tied to memory than any other sense. Perhaps it was that tight alliance that suddenly brought back all the years of roadwork that Scooter had put in without even really knowing he was doing it. The dull browns of the canyons, the heat rising off the tarmac in tiny, dizzy waves, and the far-off glint of the water joined in a blur, and Scooter picked up speed.

At first he merely closed the twenty-foot gap between the front wheel of his Ducati and the trailing rubber of the big blue Laverda. But then Scooter noticed that his father was not always picking the best lines. There were tighter ones, he saw, joining the end of one curve to the beginning of the next. He began to trace them mentally, double-checking to be sure that there was not some reason why his father was cutting wide. A moment later he passed his dad, deep and on the inside of a corner, his red-and-green motorbike laid over almost in a

match to the horizon. The engine screamed and he entered an
enraptured dance of turn after turn until his speedometer
hovered at the one-hundred-mile-per-hour mark. When he finally stopped, exhilarated and perspiring like a climbing mule,
he had to wait a full two minutes before Roman appeared
around a turn. Roman pulled up behind Scooter and stopped,
his nose twitching as if there were a fly in there, his head just
nodding and nodding and nodding.

        Scooter's newfound talents in-
creased his need for speed. He began to ride more and more
frequently, and even borrowed Roman's pickup truck so that
he could take his motorcycle to famous local racetracks with
names like Sears Point, Willow Springs, and Laguna Seca.
Sometimes, walking around the pit area, Scooter was seized by
a terrible sense that he did not belong there. He listened to the
fervor with which people discussed mechanical details. He began to classify riders by their attitudes, to learn the ring of
false modesty, insecurity, braggadocio, and pretense.

Often when Scooter went to the track with his bike, he did
not race. Instead he tried to soak up the environment like a
sponge, intellectually, as he had in his initial rides with his
father. Roman knew more than enough about motorcycles to
be able to tell when the bike returned unridden, but he also
knew enough about his son not to question him. Roman was
sure, and he had good reason to be, that it would not be long
before Scooter set tire to track.

One spring day at Willow Springs, when the high desert sky
was clear and there was nothing but a slight wind to disturb
earthly perfection, Scooter knew he was ready. He tucked a
small sprig of sagebrush he kept taped to the collar of his
racing leathers into his shirt and he entered the track. That
was also the day he began to win.

At first his successes were modest. He took first or second
place in a club race here, a sponsored national event there. He
received minor notices and was offered a free helmet by one
Japanese company and some free tires by another. Before too

long Roman himself was caught up in the thrill of Scooter's success. Very often Roman Loon would hang a sign on the door of Loon Motors, a big orange sign with black letters that said "Gone Racing." The former thief would drive the truck to the track while Scooter took a very intellectual and analytic approach, drawing pictures of the course on a big yellow legal pad, his pencil tracing perfect lines even in the bouncing cab.

Perhaps the biggest race for Southern Californians, or at least the one with the most media attention, takes place in a foreign country. It is called La Carrera and is run not on a racetrack but on the roads of the nation south of the border.

Mexico as a country can be geographically divided into three parts: the Mexican mainland, the peninsula of Yucatan, and the narrow, thousand-mile-long strip known as Baja California. Jutting out into the Pacific, Baja traps a body of water to the east, between its eastern shores and the mainland's west coast. This is the Gulf of California, noted for its fine sport fishing and long flat beaches that look dried up, as if someone had pulled the oceanic plug and let the level drop. Just over the United States border, immediately south of the most lucrative stomping grounds of Clea's husband and his baby gang, lies Tijuana, infamous stomping grounds for new members of the armed forces who have never known a woman and a place to buy cheap wrought-iron bird cages. Just south of this tourist mecca, on Baja's Pacific coast, lies Ensenada, a beer drinker's paradise and starting point of the much-publicized Mexican La Carrera motorcycle road race.

The race attracts riders from all over the Southwest and is run on highways in some places so foul that even pigs avoid them. The course transects the northern and widest part of the peninsula, leaving Ensenada and heading through a hilly section into a low desert speckled by large boulders and smeared with drifting sand.

Roman and Scooter Loon were there early and spent the night in a motel in Rosarito Beach, slightly less than halfway between Tijuana and the starting point of the race. To his father's amazement, Scooter insisted upon taking the Ducati into the motel room with them for fear of vandalism or theft. In a tiny room with a black-and-white television, tan walls, and a chocolate-brown rug, Roman Loon of Bel Air infamy prepared the bike for the race. There were long straight stretches of two-lane road for portions of the course, places where for thirty miles or more Scooter could open the throttle and let the motorcycle run full-out. Roman changed the gearing to reduce acceleration and increase top speed, and he pulled off the wheels to mount fresh tires.

"Your top end will be up from about one forty to one fifty-five," said Roman, laying down his tools and crossing his arms.

"Are you sure of the gearing?" asked Scooter, wiping the motorcycle's flank with a motel towel.

"Just wait'll you ride it," said Roman.

Scooter had heard that phrase before.

The race began with an early morning smoking gun. The riders were timed, so there was no mass start. Each motorcyclist accelerated from the line by himself while a race official pushed a stopwatch button. The roadway out of Ensenada was oily and full of potholes, and Scooter felt the Ducati quiver and shake as he gunned it over slippery ground. Thousands of Mexican men, women, and children lined the roads, squatting in the brown dust or perched atop boulders to watch the crazy gringos and the noisy machines. As Scooter went by he thought how very foreign it was to see people squat. He tried to think of the last time he had seen somebody squat in America and couldn't. As he shifted gears he wondered where the squatting line was. He wondered whether the border was the squatting line, and how close squatters and non-squatters came to each other. He wondered if it was close enough for them to call to each other without phones.

Near a little town named Santo Tomas a rider died in front

of the mistoed Loon. The pack of riders had just come down out of some hills and begun a great thin straightaway. Scooter knew that the road would not curve for some time because there were no road signs. In Baja every single curve, no matter how insignificant, is denoted by a yellow sign with a black representation of the turn. Scooter looked as far ahead as he could, moving past slower riders, but he saw no signs. He did see small dots moving on the road below, and he assumed from such a distance that they were race fans along the course.

At speeds greater than one hundred miles per hour, one's eyes have nothing on which to fix and perspective is lost. The faster one goes, the narrower the road appears, until at 150 miles per hour it seems nothing but an infinite black pencil line stretching to the horizon. Too, at such speeds maneuvering is best done with the slightest wishful push or tug, as even the sudden appearance of an elbow out of the airstream can cause a radical change in direction.

When the goat appeared suddenly in the middle of the roadway, he was an utter surprise to Scooter and the rider in front of him. The animal had been hidden in a small dip in the road, invisible from more than fifty feet away. Such dips were not characteristic of the Baja flatland, but they did exist.

The rider tried to swerve and avoid the goat, but succeeded only in upsetting the balance of his English machine so that his front wheel struck the animal sideways instead of square-on. The beast exploded in a shower of intestine and skin, and Scooter could think only of popping a birthday-party balloon when he was a small boy. The animal's recent remains made the roadway slick, and Loon skittered through. When he succeeded in bringing the Ducati to a halt and rushed back, the rider was already dead, his neck broken at a grotesque angle, one eye bulging, the other closed.

Scooter had never seen a dead person before. He walked numbly back along the track and waved his arms so that the other riders would slow down, then he bent and pulled the rider off the road by hooking his eleven fingers underneath the man's armpits. He noticed that there was no blood, and that the man had been perspiring heavily. Next he dragged the pieces of the dead man's old Norton to the side of the road, got back on his own bike, and continued the race.

Once back up to speed, Scooter had time to evaluate his feelings. He recognized that he was numb and detached, as if a little homunculus had been excised from his person and was sitting outside him on a cloud, arms akimbo, watching with a knowing look. He talked to himself in an icy, calm way, and he rode his Ducati with both the ferocity of a demon and the icy calm of a surgeon.

The farther he went, the faster he rode. Soon he had opened the motorcycle to full throttle and was threading his way through the riders in front of him as if they were standing still. He picked and weaved and picked and weaved, all the while talking to a little man on a cloud in front of him. He thought about the dead rider, wondered if he had a family that would miss him, a mother or a father, a sister or a brother.

As Scooter Loon descended to the finish of the race, the great salt flats of San Felipe stretched out in front of him, looking for all the world as if the starving people of Mexico had ravaged the sea life and slurped the tide dry in their hunger. Scooter crossed the finish line to waves and cheers, and he looked around to find Roman. The older man was there, with a single finger up in the air, jumping and screaming about something, but for a moment, as he took off his helmet and his sweat got in his eyes, all Scooter could see was a party balloon going pop, pop, pop.

11

Biji's dreams of being an actress were not spawned by an appetite for fame and excess. Even at the dreamy age of eighteen she did not give a whit about strolling down Rodeo Drive and being suddenly beset by photographers. Rather, Biji's ambitions were much more exact, exactness being a characteristic she shared with her misfingered kinsman. Their shared traits were few, however, because overall Scooter Loon was introverted and cool and Biji Steinberg was passionate and self-centered. Biji knew that she should be an actress because she had an ability to project herself into any situation, to actually fear and love a role. She thought she could change color and form according to the script, and she was right.

To Murray Feldman, Biji was another Jewish-American princess whose daddy he owed a favor. Murray was too smart to let this kind of thing happen to him often, but nobody living in Hollywood can avoid such situations altogether. They are part of the stuff of power and life.

It was Murray's job to recognize someone special when he saw them, and even before he had Biji read lines the producer knew he was onto something. He also felt a funny twitching between his legs.

"I'd rather my father didn't watch," said Biji, looking straight at lawyer Adam, who sat in Murray's leather chair swelling with pride at Biji's every word.

"Does he make you nervous?" asked Murray.

"Not at all," said Biji. "He's my father. How could he make me nervous? I know he loves me."

"Well then?" said the father of two mutants.

"It's because he loves me so much that I worry," said Biji.

"You won't disappoint me, honey," said Adam.

"It's not that at all," Biji said, turning to the producer. "I'm just worried he's going to bug the hell out of you about the test. 'Some screen test, huh, Murray?' or something like that. On the phone, in the elevator, over cocktails. I just want you to make up your own mind, Mr. Feldman."

Murray stared at her a long moment and then dismissed Steinberg with a wave of his hand. "Get lost, Adam," he said. "Biji and I have work to do."

The screen test involved reading some lines from a movie that Biji had never seen. It was called *Anaconda Weekend* and told the story of a pair of coeds lost in the Brazilian jungle after their tour boat went down in the Amazon River.

"I've never seen a movie script before," said Biji, looking up at Murray from the pages, "but this has to be the worst one around."

"Precisely," said Murray. "That's why I gave it to you. If you can make something of it, then you really can be a star."

Biji leafed through the pages for a moment and then shook her head.

"I don't think so, Mr. Feldman," she said. "If this is the test, then I fail. Even a great actress can't make something out of nothing. I need good lines to give a good reading. I really appreciate you giving me this chance, even though I know you owe my dad for something, so I want to do well for you. Why don't you let me read you something from one of Jane Fonda's roles?"

"Something from one of Jane Fonda's roles," murmured Feldman. "Something from one of Jane Fonda's roles," he shouted to his assistant.

After the reading, which had Feldman completely mesmerized, Biji was sent in for camera work. She was photographed from many angles, and in a host of costumes that fit her so well Biji wondered whether Sharon had snuck into her closet and sent the studio some of Biji's clothes so that they would know the exact size. This was, of course, exactly what had happened.

It seemed that lighting had no effect on Biji's glow. Under a red bulb, wearing black leather pants, she looked like a classy whore. Under blue-white light with a paisley dress and an umbrella, her hair braided, and a little rouge applied, Biji looked like she could charm Santa out of Donner or Blitzen. Murray was fascinated by her quick changes, dubbing her "the chameleon" when talking to his makeup crew.

When the test was over, and role bits of Biji were indelibly captured on film for later review, Murray had Biji put on her street clothes and meet him in his office. Biji was perspiring from the lights, and Murray found that her faint odor aroused him.

"Well," he said, rubbing his damp palms together, "I have to tell you, Biji, that you have real talent."

Biji just looked at the carpet.

"Suddenly humble and demure?" chuckled Feldman. "From what I've seen, it isn't like you."

"Isn't this the part where I'm supposed to be modest and cast down my eyes?" asked Biji.

"You know," said Feldman, "I think it's going to be me that bugs your father and not the other way around."

Biji just smiled.

Early the next morning, when Sharon and Adam thought she was off to an early class, Biji drove her big green convertible Caddy back to the office of the baby doctor. She got out and walked into the building with the dark brown windows. The waiting room was empty, and the elderly nurse rose when she entered. The doctor was nowhere in sight.

"Come into the examination room," said the nurse, "and put on this robe." She handed Biji a light blue gown made of tissue paper. Biji was so nervous that when she tried to put it on, she ripped a hole and exposed her belly. She carefully folded her clothes and laid them out on the chair. They looked, she thought, like the person wearing them had just deflated and blown away. Biji was sitting with her feet hanging over the examining table, just like the doctor had the morning

before, when the nurse reappeared. She stared at the hole over
Biji's midriff.

"He doesn't go in that way, honey," she said. "He goes in
through your private parts."

Biji mustered her most withering stare.

"I know that," she said. "I was just trying to put it on and
the paper ripped. For what I'm sure you guys charge, you
could at least get cotton robes."

The nurse pursed her lips and departed, to be replaced a
moment later by the kidnapping gynecologist.

"Have you eaten anything this morning?" he asked.

"Nothing," said Biji.

"Lie down and put your feet in the stirrups," he said.

Biji lay back and began to count green Cadillacs in her
mind's eye as the doctor maneuvered her into the precise position he wanted and then administered anesthesia. Biji kept
staring at the ceiling, trying not to think of anything but the
tiny green cars she was attempting to project onto the stucco.
She could feel the doctor's instruments inside her, and a dull
pain began. She listened to the mechanical slurping of the suc-
tion machine.

The metal nozzle of the machine especially designed to dis-
lodge and swallow incipient human life had a sharp edge. It
was this sharp edge that punctured both horns of Biji's eighteen-year-old uterus when the nurse suddenly knocked on the
door and the doctor jumped. The curtain that had kept Biji's
sensations dull was lifted and she cried out in pain.

It would be difficult to prove that the doctor's hands slipped
deliberately. Though he feared and disliked Biji, he did not
consciously wish to cause her harm. Immediately, however,
there was blood everywhere. Biji could see rivulets out of the
corner of her eye as the fluid made its way to the drain on the
floor. She could hear the doctor cursing, too, and the nurse
hustling back and forth with drains, sponges, and sharp in-
takes of breath. The activity seemed to go on forever, and then
everything turned the color of a shallow, tropical sea.

Adam Steinberg's Yale buddy, the same baby doctor who
had delivered Scooter almost directly from Sharon's loins to

Roman Loon's thieving hands, was in deep, deep trouble. In his mind, as he tried to salvage Biji's shredded reproductive organs, he was calculating the money he had spent on malpractice insurance over the years. He was trying to assess the size of the lawsuit that he knew lawyer Adam would levy upon him. He decided that no matter how good Adam was at his trade, and the doctor feared he was excellent, his malpractice coverage would protect him, and the premiums would prove to be an outstanding investment. For several moments he considered letting Biji die, but the nurse was watching his every move, and she wasn't as loyal as his darling Clea.

The doctor stemmed the tide of blood with cautery, but the damage was so severe that he was unsure he could effect a permanent repair. He directed the nurse to cancel his other morning appointments and mind the phone, and as soon as she had left the room, the doctor made sure that Biji's innards were intact enough to produce the hormones of womanhood, even though she would never be able to bear a child.

To be rendered utterly sterile at the age of eighteen by a doctor's bungling was certainly a tragedy of considerable magnitude. The doctor decided then and there, however, not to say a word about it to anyone. Mentally he wagered that Biji would never refer to the episode, and would not, he hoped, know the difference for years to come. It was a decision that could not take into account all the twists and turns of Biji's later life, and it was a decision rendered under duress.

Much later, when Biji awoke, she was in great pain and felt like there was a hollowness beneath her navel that had never been there before.

"How big was it?" she asked the doctor.

The gynecologist brought his fingers together until they outlined a circle about the size of a walnut.

"Did it have feelings?" asked Biji.

The doctor shook his head.

"Could you tell whether it would have been a boy or a girl?" asked Biji, trying to sit up and falling back weakly.

"I want you to lie here for a couple of hours," said the doctor, covering her with a blanket.

"You said I would be able to leave right afterwards," said Biji.

"You lost a little more blood than I expected," said the doctor.

"Could you?"

"Could I what?"

"Tell if it would have been a boy or a girl," Biji repeated.

"No," said the doctor. "I really couldn't."

"I feel very hollow," said Biji.

"Perfectly understandable," said the doctor. "It will pass."

As soon as he left the room the teenage sister of Scooter Loon grabbed at the bloody sheets and covered her mouth so nobody would hear her cry.

When Biji returned home she was still in considerable pain, and she looked as white as typewriter paper. Sharon was naturally concerned.

"You look terrible," she told Biji as the teenager collapsed on the bed.

"I don't need you to tell me how terrible I look," Biji suddenly screamed. "I don't need you for anything. I don't need anybody at all. Just leave me alone!" With this she crumpled up in the same position as her recently removed fetus and began to shake with sobs.

Sharon just stared as if she had been slapped and Adam appeared in the doorway.

"I just got a call from Murray Feldman," he said gently, staring with bewilderment first at his daughter and then at his wife, "and he doesn't think you look terrible at all."

Biji kept her head buried in her pillow.

"He says you're going to be a star. He says you're like a chameleon, the way you can change from role to role. He's already got a job filming a commercial for you. Congratulations, honey."

Biji just moaned.

"I still say she looks terrible," said Sharon, closing the bedroom door with a shake of her head.

"She's going to be in a commercial," whispered Adam.

At that instant they both thought of Scooter Loon.

"I wonder if Bernard . . ." Sharon began.

Adam Steinberg put his finger to his lips and closed his eyes so tight he saw stars.

12

Genetics and environment usually conspire to lay down certain rules for life. Most people are not blessed with a plenitude of career choices but rather tend in the direction where skill and opportunity lie. Writers write because they must, mathematicians compute because everything else seems imprecise, and businessmen hustle because they don't know any other way. Since Scooter could do anything from play soccer to solve nuclear physics problems, he had a difficult time choosing a career path. While his friends were partying their senior year away, the last eight months at the University of California were tough stuff for the brainy Loon.

"Definitely medical school," said Marian Loon.

"Don't be ridiculous," said Roman. "Doctors don't race motorcycles."

"Maybe he shouldn't be racing motorcycles," she replied.

"I could always be the first," said Scooter. "We could paint the words *Dr. Speed* on my gas tank."

"Dr. Speed," Roman mused.

"Just kidding," said Scooter.

"How about *Harefoot*?" suggested his mother.

Father and son just stared at her.

"Because he's so fast," she said.

"I don't see what's wrong with helping me run the shop during the week and racing on weekends," said Roman.

"I really enjoy the time with you," said Scooter, "but I think I should try and develop some kind of career."

"If you want a career, I have an idea for you," Roman began.

"Forget that," Marian interrupted.

"I don't think I have the nerve to burgle," said Scooter.

"You cross Mexican ground on two skinny little patches of rubber at a hundred and fifty miles per hour and you tell me you don't have nerve?" said Roman.

"It's a different kind of nerve."

"It's got nothing to do with nerve," Marian said firmly. "Your father didn't have the education and opportunity that you have."

"He doesn't have eleven fingers and eleven toes either," said Scooter.

The older Loons looked at each other.

"How about law school?" said Marian.

"How could I go to law school with a thief for a father?" Scooter said as gently as he could.

"Former thief," said Roman.

"Business school then," said Marian.

"He doesn't need to go to school for that," said the cat burglar. "Look how well the bike shop is doing."

"Business school," mused Scooter.

In the end Scooter made application to Yale, Harvard, Stanford, and the University of California branch in Los Angeles. He was admitted everywhere and was forced to consider long and hard. Harvard was a good name, he thought, but from what he heard of Cambridge, Massachusetts, it was a carnival town. He didn't think his clothes were fancy enough to make it at Stanford, and Los Angeles didn't excite him, so he ended up choosing Yale. When he went for his interview it was cold and raining, but the buildings were impressive and serious and even the trees had character.

It took time and effort for him to convince Roman that he could live on the scholarship money and stipend and that he would be back to California just as soon as the two-year course was over. Marian knew she would miss him terribly, but was elated that he was striking out on his own. She felt that great things were in store for her stolen boy.

* * *

Despite his intellect and education, Scooter Loon had a fairly narrow world view. This stemmed from the fact that, except to race his Ducati in Mexico, he had never been outside of Southern California. Yale University was a mecca for accomplished individuals and scholars from around the globe, and Scooter Loon found himself instantly transported into what seemed a bazaar in a farming country. The former Bernard Steinberg found bright, exotic-looking, and interesting people everywhere.

Outside Yale's Gothic wrought-iron gates, New Haven, Connecticut, is largely a black ghetto. Scooter Loon was intelligent enough to lack prejudice and naive enough to believe that he would be accepted in turn. The first Saturday after he arrived in New Haven, Scooter took his Ducati and set out to explore New Haven streets. It was late summer, and the smog from the harbor hung heavy over the potholed streets. Waves of heat rose from the engine and washed over Scooter's legs.

Cruising the city on his bike, he felt increasingly uneasy, aware that the flashy machine with the loud exhaust was out of place and was drawing undue attention. He reached a red light and drew to a halt next to a battered blue station wagon.

"Yo. How fast does that thing go?" a youth with broad fleshy arms called, leaning out of the car window until he was inches from the Bel Air boy.

"Fast enough," Scooter said.

The driver of the car eased it forward and to the right until it nearly brushed Scooter's leg. Several old black men with cigarette-stained fingers watched from a bench at a gas station at the corner. The car edged closer, and Scooter had to move the bike slightly with his feet. The passenger grinned.

"Faster than this old heap?" he said.

"Unless you've got a rocket engine under the hood," said Scooter.

The light turned green and the car rocketed away, smoking tires until the world was misty blue. Scooter let the Ducati's clutch out gently and proceeded from the stoplight at a snail's pace.

At the next light the car was there again.

Scooter raised the face shield on his helmet so that he could be perfectly understood.

"I could have embarrassed you back there," he said.

"Is that right?" the passenger grinned. "Why didn't you?"

"It's like taking candy from a baby," said Scooter.

"It's like taking candy from a baby," said the passenger to the driver, nodding with mock solemnity.

"Do you know East Rock Road?" the driver called to Scooter from the left side of the car.

"No."

"Would you like to race there—your bike, our candy?"

"Does the road have turns in it?" asked Scooter Loon, winner of La Carrera and other famous road races.

"Sure," said the passenger.

"Won't take long," added the driver.

"I know," said Scooter Loon.

East Rock Road is a favorite New Haven driving course. The narrow two-lane winds up the side of a small hill and arrives at a flat parking spot on top where teenage couples come to neck. Going up the hill, there are turns bordered by rock on the right. Coming down, a misplaced wheel will jump clear off into space.

Scooter tailed the blue wagon to the base of the rock, where the road began to wind up the hill. The road was not wide enough for the two vehicles to race side by side, unless Scooter rode the opposing lane.

"How do you want to work this?" asked Scooter.

"Whoever gets to the top first wins the race," called the driver of the blue station wagon.

"I know that," Scooter said. "I mean about the lanes. I don't want to ride in the wrong lane."

"Why don't you just take the candy from this baby and pass us right away?" leered the passenger.

There are times when even someone as cool and modest as Scooter Loon can be an ass. To his credit, Scooter realized his mistake the moment he had made the baby remark, and looking ahead at the twisty lines of the unfamiliar road, he knew he was about to be very sorry.

The car tore away faster than seemed possible, and as he cranked open the throttle on the Ducati it crossed his mind that the youths must be using nitrous oxide injection. Nitrous oxide, the same gas that causes dental patients to laugh at pulsing walls and play space pilot, also happens to instantly double the horsepower of a gasoline engine when introduced into the combustion chamber. Scooter knew that he could be battling as much as six hundred horsepower at the car's rear wheel.

The Italian engine strained and whined and the front wheel came off the ground as Bernard Steinberg groused through the gears with a vengeance. On a straightaway that led into a blind turn, Scooter made his move to pass the car and take the lead.

The driver of the car had been watching Scooter in his rearview mirror. As soon as he saw the motorcycle's front tire swing out and into the passing lane, he swung, too, placing his car directly in Scooter's path. Dr. Speed dropped back, and then tried again a moment later. When the car swung left Scooter saw a space to the right, and decided to pass the car on the inside.

Despite his racing successes, Scooter's riding and his personality were not characterized by recklessness and bravado. He won at the racetrack because he took an intellectual approach and because he spent hours and hours studying the lines through turns and knowing the strengths and weaknesses of his competitors. He was a master of visualization, picturing himself running the course over and over in his mind's eye. The impromptu race with the New Haven boys was not the type of race to which Scooter was accustomed. Scooter had never seen East Rock before and had not even once raced an "injected" Chevrolet.

The space between the blue Chevy and the red granite of East Rock was tight, and it diminished quickly as the boy drivers swung back and tried to pin Scooter to stone. The adrenaline rose in his throat and the lone Loon opened the throttle wide. The Ducati screamed and Scooter squirted through the space, taking the lead and cutting angry lines through the series of turns that wound to the top.

Once there, Scooter flicked his kickstand down and came off the bike. He was angrier than he had ever been in his life. He watched the corner that lead to the lookout, waiting for a confrontation with the nitro boys, wondering what it would be like to use his fists on foreign soil. He waited for the better part of an hour, his breath gradually returning to normal, the sky turning orange with day's end. The boys never showed up.

The smoggy New Haven skyline spread before him like a dirty map. He could see Yale and the buildings that housed his graduate school, peeks of brown stone between the trees. He imagined a dark-robed don standing by the rusty rail of the East Rock lookout, his hand outstretched, as if to congratulate Mr. Scooter Loon on his initiation to the world where dad did not wait at the finish line.

13

That autumn in New Haven was Bernard Steinberg's first. Dropping leaves, the smell of burning hickory, and a certain briskness in the air all awakened sensibilities that Scooter had long gauzed over. When he left California, Scooter also left behind him a semi-opaque shield that covered certain emotions. Plainly put, Scooter was unlaid. In all his twenty-two years, even with his gonads running amuck through puberty, Bernard Steinberg had experienced nothing more than schoolboy crushes. In New Haven some restless little imp stirred in the man, and Scooter's eyes began to roam over the myriads of exotic women that inhabited the Yale campus.

In a class called The Psychology of Power, affectionately known as "Boss 101," Scooter became aware of a Persian girl who smelled like a sweet flower from another planet. Her name, he noticed on the inside of her textbook, was Faranak. For days Scooter sat directly behind her, taking in the curve of her, the way she sat, and the shifts and flow of her shoulders when she wrote or looked up at the blackboard. Her body was more lush and rounded than the American ideal, with a stretching tightness to it that suggested she exercised often, which she didn't. Sometimes Scooter caught himself with his eyes closed, inhaling her perfume. Her hair was very black and as shiny as the surface of the sea sometimes gets when there are things floating there and the sun is just right.

Scooter, who fancied himself a very logical and self-controlled individual, developed what he himself recognized as a little obsession. In the first week Faranak became the embodiment of all the fantasies he had never had. Because she was the stuff of his nightly dreams, he was afraid to see her face. He began to come to class consistently late so that he would always arrive after she did and never be forced to look at the front of her. When class broke he stared hard at his textbook until she walked by.

Three weeks after he first noticed her Scooter gathered the nerve to sit to the side of her for a glimpse at her profile. He gritted his teeth hard, the way he did when entering a fast-sweeping corner that he could not see all the way through. His first look was obscured by her hair, which fell down like a teasing curtain and afforded him only a glance at the tip of her nose. Thankfully, she was no Cyrano. Her proboscis was gently rounded and seemed not to stick out too far. When she raised her head to copy something from the front of the room, Scooter gained a peek at a flash of cheek. Her skin was brown, as if she had just returned from a vacation in the sun. Scooter recognized her name as Middle Eastern, though he did not find out until later that she was Persian.

For her part Faranak was not only aware of Scooter's timorous but steadily increasing attentions, she was amused by them. At first she could not believe that somebody could come late to class and leave early every day, and she presumed that Scooter had a scheduling conflict. His interest dawned on her one day when she saw him staring intently at his textbook when she walked by. The book was the wrong one for the class and it was upside down.

If Faranak had been Biji, she would have ambushed Scooter in the hall or just inside the door. She would have told him face-to-face that he was acting like a thirteen-year-old idiot and asked him if he had a problem of some kind. But Persian women are not raised like the daughter of Sharon and Adam Steinberg, and Faranak was from Teheran, not Bel Air. As a result she kept her observations to herself and waited patiently for Scooter Loon to make the first move. With a Persian woman's camel-like resolve, Faranak determined not to return his glance when he sat next to her.

Like houseplants that are ripped out and repotted, people tend to anchor themselves and grow in familiar directions wherever they are. Scooter's schedule at Yale University's

School of Organization and Management was therefore much the same as it had been while attending college in Santa Barbara. The difference, of course, was that he was not working at Loon Motors. Accustomed to completing his studies at odd and limited hours, and with a brain that gained him honors in minutes, Scooter found himself with much time on his hands. Some of this he spent tinkering with his Ducati in the garage of the tiny red house he rented by the railroad tracks. As the weather grew colder, however, his interest in riding diminished, and with the first early October frost, Scooter drained the bike, lubed it, and prepared it for the long winter as Roman had told him to do.

Scooter had not been bored since the very early years of his life when, in the soundproof nursery built by the loving hands of Roman Loon, he had stared for hours at the same revolving pieces of metal and paper and what seemed to his dim memory to be a dead bug. Being both bored and obsessed, young Loon began to follow Faranak around.

Lacking Roman's tailing talents, Scooter's attempts to conceal his tail were clumsy and doomed to failure. Faranak spotted him nearly everywhere she went. One evening she saw him in the cafeteria, sitting at a table, shivering in a leather jacket, eating microwave popcorn, and trying not to look at her. She did not know that he was afraid to commit himself to the food line in case she suddenly left the hall.

Yale University, in blatant mimicry of venerable English institutions, is divided into twelve residential colleges. The idea is that students are more likely to flourish in a social environment that is cozy and does not overwhelm. The university experience is scaled down so that each student dines with the same people nightly, lives in a dormitory with the same people for three of the four undergraduate years, and ultimately nucleates his social life within the confines of the assigned college. Though taking a business school course, Faranak was still an undergraduate. Scooter Loon did not belong in the dining hall at Faranak's residential college, and when he began to appear there on a regular basis, he stuck out like a fork with mangled tines. His attentions were so obvious to everybody that Faranak's girlfriends began to tease her. Scooter did not notice.

The vast number of books in Yale's library are arranged in stacks that go up into a great Gothic tower. There is a musky smell up there, and the light is yellow. These are the bowels of the library. Very serious students, many of whom later have nervous breakdowns or come to think that they are somebody they aren't, spend studying time there. Faranak, not because she was driven or neurotic, but because she came from another land and greatly valued the opportunity afforded her at Yale, spent many hours each night in these stacks.

One evening Scooter followed her there from dinner. He climbed the stairs on the tips of his rubber-soled shoes so that she would not hear him, and he watched from the next narrow aisle, his face only three feet from hers, as she positioned herself in a tiny corner of the stacks. She folded her legs and propped her head against a shelf, a textbook on her knees. He stared at her high cheekbones and black eyes and realized that he had seen her before, in little glimpses and takes.

Faranak had long been told that Semitic people have special faculties given them by Allah in the days when they still flew around on carpets. Whatever the sense involved, Faranak all at once knew she was being watched, and she looked up in an instant to meet Scooter's eye through the shelving. She smiled sweetly at him and crooked her little finger in a beckon. When she saw that he was frozen dumb, she rounded the aisle only to find young Loon nonchalantly thumbing through a tattered blue volume entitled *On the Construction of Wooden Ships of War*.

"Great book," were his first words to her.

She came to his side, took the book out of his hands, and replaced it in the slightly too-narrow space from which he had taken it.

"You are reading upside down."

"I'm dyslexic," said Scooter.

"What does this mean?"

"It means I have to read things upside down."

"Do you have a special interest in"—she paused for a moment to read the title of the book—"wooden ships of war?"

"I'm hoping to join the navy," said Scooter.

"Is that why you are in business school?"

"The navy is big business," Scooter said, feeling himself getting weaker from the nearness of her.

"I have heard that in this country the war people will pay for you to go to school. Is that what they are doing for you?"

"Actually, I am on a scholarship," said Scooter.

"So they are paying for you to study here?"

"Yes," said Scooter, "but not the navy."

"So they are paying for your school now, but they will not pay for you when you are in the navy, sailing on ships?"

Scooter became terribly flustered. "The navy has nothing to do with me right now," he said.

"So you are not a spy?"

"No."

"Then why are you following me all over the campus?" said Faranak.

If Scooter had been capable of autocombustion at that moment, he would have burst into scorching, embarrassed flames.

"I wanted to talk to you," he said.

Biji Steinberg would have humiliated Scooter with an acerbic retort guaranteed to bring him to his knees, but Faranak was not that way.

"Talk to me now," she said.

Scooter stared at her very full lips.

"Where do you come from?" he said.

"I am from Iran," she said, moving closer to him.

It can be fairly said that Persian men have two body types. They are either very skinny with long wrists, hands, and fingers, or they are squat and move as if they were forever trying to get lower to the ground. Faranak was fascinated by all the new male physiques she had seen since coming to school at New Haven, and she appraised Scooter Loon close up. She noticed that while he hid one hand behind his back rather awkwardly, his body was in the same perfect proportions she saw in the *Playgirl* magazine she read every night but hid behind her dresser so that her roommates wouldn't know.

"I am from California," said Scooter Loon.

"Why are you standing that way?" said Faranak.

"What way?" said Scooter, burying his six-fingered hand deeper into his hind pocket.

"Twisted the way you are?" said Faranak.

Scooter Loon may have been the master of his previous impulses, but a beautiful woman with perfect skin, full lips, and breasts that strained her clothing standing inches from him was more than he could stand.

"I like your perfume," he said.

"I am not wearing any." Faranak smiled.

"But you smell like flowers," said Scooter.

Faranak raised her chin high so that her neck was exposed.

"Sniff me," she said.

Because she was half a foot shorter than Scooter, exposing her throat brought the Persian girl's mouth invitingly close.

"I believe I will," he said, taking his hand from his pocket and gently pulling her close.

To Scooter, who had gone through nearly a quarter century of life without a woman's touch, Faranak's skin fairly danced with electric charges. He felt his knees get weak as his eyes closed and their lips met. Faranak was not lying when she said that she was wearing no perfume. She was wearing toilet water. The scent of it became stronger as she melted into Scooter, and for a time he thought he would drown in it. Breathing that way, with his skin on fire, the furthest thing in the world from Bernard Steinberg's mind was that his sister Biji was soon to be on the cover of every entertainment and women's magazine in the country.

14

FBI Special Agent Niles Grosbeak was a thin and brittle man with long bones and a crusty demeanor. It is somewhat cliché for lawmen to become obsessed with apprehending elusive suspects, and Niles strove never to reveal that the activities of the baby gang that had stolen Bernard Steinberg and the child of the Japanese consul in San Francisco were the focus of his every waking minute.

In the more than twenty years that the baby gang had been active, Grosbeak had been enormously successful in apprehending a surfeit of scum. He had cuffed disgruntled husbands who defied court orders and tracked down vindictive babysitters who had dreamed of crumpling families. Yet in the long run, despite rounding up even an occasional repeat offender, Niles had yet to get to the kernel of most of the baby stealing and resale in California. A quarter of a century is a long time to pursue a nefarious cadre that you cannot prove even exists, and the FBI had long since forced Grosbeak to officially terminate the Bel Air and San Francisco inquiries.

Failure and frustration had extracted Niles's optimism and spirit as surely as a dentist pulls a fractured tooth. But tenacity was the special agent's middle name, and every time he felt the urge to abandon the project, he awakened in the middle of the night with a terrible dream.

In the dream Niles saw the bright green seas about a small tropical island as if from a helicopter hovering slow and low. An enormous outrigger canoe was tracing the shoreline of the island, paralleling the reef. Thick, bronzed, island men dipped hand-hewn paddles into the water and drew back strongly to spread spray. In the bottom of the canoe, with a coarse cloth around its middle, lay the stolen Bernard Steinberg, his eleven fingers waving, his eleven toes wriggling. His pale baby skin was reddening and blistering from the equatorial sun, and his movements were growing ever feebler.

The silent, unseen chopper that carried FBI Agent Grosbeak swung away from the boat and toward the island in the background. There, tucked back from the shore, nestled in the waving arms of palms, was a small camp ringed with barbed wire and patrolled by neo-Nazi types wearing khaki greens and swastikas. Children of various ages roamed the compound, some tied together with twine in lines, others free but with dull eyes. Niles recognized the children. He knew each and every face from his FBI files and from the lovingly assembled family photo albums that he had been shown for over twenty years by distraught parents.

Niles tried to swoop in and get a better view, but as he came closer he realized that the guards were all looking up, aiming machine guns and antiaircraft equipment at his naked, sleeping face. With the first burst of fire, Niles reached his hands out, screamed, and woke up. Sometimes the dream was so intense that the policeman found his elbows locked and sore. As a well-trained agent, Niles knew the psychological origin of the recurring dream and was well aware of the source of his metaphorical helplessness. He tried to cure himself of the dream by reading funny books with silly pictures before he went to sleep, and even sat propped against the pillows before retiring and spoke to himself out loud, analyzing his feelings and telling himself how ridiculous they were. One day he bought a laugh sack, a bag with a simple tape player that sounded a man in hysterical laughter at the press of a button, and brought it home for underneath his pillow. The first night it hurt his ear so much, he awoke looking like a prizefighter, and the second he threw it against the wall in disgust at three fifteen in the morning. Then he fell asleep and had the dream again.

The dream was a permutation of one of Grosbeak's early missions for the Bureau. Grosbeak had raided a drug-refining operation off the Georgia coast and found whole families, including small children, living off the laboratory proceeds.

There had been no gunfire and no Nazis, but Grosbeak had thought long and hard about the future of children who had grown up refining cocaine. Over a long period of time these continued interruptions in his nightly sleep patterns nearly ruined Grosbeak, but in the end he learned to cope with them by doing the best he possibly could during his working day. He applied extra after-hours computer time to the kidnappings and garnered men and services at every possible opportunity. He was convinced, correctly, that he was dealing with a particular organized criminal element, but his mistake lay in assuming that all the crimes he was investigating were committed by the baby gang that had stolen Scooter Loon. He was trying, in short, to tie together crimes that could not be tied together, and it was not until he began to narrow the field that he could make progress.

When the leader of the baby gang lost Clea to Sharon's gynecologist, he had what can only be termed a wildly psychotic episode in which he drove his Ferrari convertible around West Los Angeles with a pair of his wife's underpants on his head, his eyes peeking through the leg holes. He made it nearly from Westwood to the ocean, a distance of several miles, before a sea wind combined with the air behind his windshield and caused the panties to turn clockwise about his head. The gangster lost visual contact with the road just long enough to slam broadside into a county sheriff's vehicle that was taking the scenic route back to the station. The arresting officer was fairly accustomed to L.A. loonies, and since he received nothing more than two bruised ribs, he managed a congenial smile as he placed the reckless driver under arrest.

Back at the sheriff's office, the baby-gang leader was fingerprinted. Fear had broken through his despair at losing Clea's bedtime company, and he knew how to play on the heartstrings of even the most hardened copper.

"You see these panties," he told the deputy who was typing up his arrest sheet.

"I see 'em."

"Can you guess who they belong to?"

"I hope not you," said the lawman.

"They belong to my wife," said the gangster.

"Ah-ha."

"My soon-to-be-ex-wife."

"Ah-ha."

"My wife, whom I brought up from the gutter. She just left me for a Beverly Hills gynecologist who she says has magic fingers."

"What do you mean brought up from the gutter?" asked the cop absently as he paused to correct a typo.

"She was a hooker, a common whore, what do you think I mean?"

"Bet she was good in the sack, huh?" said the young deputy, typing slower and slower.

"Why do you think I'm driving around with her underwear on my head? I'm dying. I mean, it didn't matter how tired I was. It didn't matter if I thought I didn't have enough energy to change a light bulb. She would get her hands on me and . . ."

In the end the baby-gang leader was bailed out by one of his cronies and a small fine was levied. His fingerprints went on file, but there was nothing to charge him with other than reckless endangerment, a charge that the presiding judge reduced to a speeding ticket when he heard the sorry circumstances from a certain sympathetic young deputy.

Shocked by this minor but near disastrous brush with the law, the baby-gang leader regained much of his former piss and vinegar, and in the ensuing several years reformed his gang with a vengeance and went after California's young once more. It was the string of middle-class kidnappings and the discovery of a missing infant alone and clueless in a banana crate near the docks at the Los Angeles port of San Pedro that gave Niles Grosbeak the scent once more. At least, Niles knew now, the baby gang could bumble.

15

The career of Biji Steinberg was initially tethered to the somewhat scurrile appetite of Murray Feldman. Being a heterosexual director who had spent considerable years in Hollywood, Feldman was jaded to the point of outright abusiveness and hostility when it came to his physical relations with women. He craved newness and excitement so badly that he challenged each new partner as if she were a heavyweight contender.

Murray's feelings for Biji were more complex than his hots for the usual budding starlet. This was because he was good enough at his business to recognize real talent when he saw it and because, professionally, he had to face Adam Steinberg on occasion. Murray had immediately perceived that Biji Steinberg was not the sort of woman whom one jerked around. She was blunt, she appreciated bluntness, and Murray could be as blunt as a paint roller when he had to. He made his move, or more correctly he proposed his deal, when Biji was busy shooting her first commercial, a toothpaste ad set on a forty-foot sailboat off the California coast.

"Do you always come on commercial shoots?" Biji asked Murray as she peeled off a yellow sweatshirt top to reveal a Day-Glo orange bikini and her tan and perfect skin.

Murray sat on the edge of the cockpit with his feet on cushions and his stubby legs crossed. The sail was flapping with the wind and the boom, though tied, moved back and forth, causing Biji to duck. Murray did not have to duck because he was so short and because he was sitting down.

"Sometimes," said Murray. "Not always."

Biji knew that a producer as important as Murray Feldman had no business on a television commercial shoot. She knew that Murray was involved in forty-million-dollar feature films and that he mingled at will with the Hollywood ruling caste. To her credit, she also knew that he was on board to see her undressed.

"Okay, Biji," said one of the cameramen, beginning to get his equipment ready, "look in this direction and let's see that gorgeous set of chompers."

"Chompers?" said Biji.

"Teeth," said Murray Feldman, never taking his eyes off of Biji's scantily clad figure.

"Thanks for clearing that up," said Biji.

The sailboat cleared the same harbor where the now famous "banana bantling" had been strangely recovered in a banana crate and aimed north for the waters off Malibu Beach, where the filming would take place looking east toward the shoreline. The water wind fanned Biji's auburn locks into a wild mop, with stringy bits forming a madwoman halo. Biji didn't know it then, but this witchy look was absolutely torturing Murray Feldman. He had a fondness for black lipstick and unruly hair that went beyond preference. Leaning back against the fiberglass boatpiece, Murray got so aroused he had to close his eyes.

"This angle all right, Mr. Feldman?"

"Any angle is all right," Murray mumbled.

"I beg your pardon, sir?"

"Change the bathing suit to one that's not so tight," said Murray with his eyes still closed.

Biji was puzzled. "The set directions call for an orange suit," she said.

"They also call for a five-foot-five-inch blonde," said the producer.

"I thought that producers didn't get involved in this kind of detail," Biji said, sitting down so close to him that the faint hairs on her thighs brushed his light blue leisure suit.

"Go change," said Feldman faintly, not looking at her.

Below deck, Biji found an entire wardrobe of swimsuits and leisure wear, including rubberized gear for scuba diving. Biji had never tried on a wet suit before. She stripped off her bikini and stepped into a short-sleeved jacket. Struggling with the zipper, she did not notice Murray Feldman until he sat down heavily on the hatchway stairs.

"What are you doing?" said Scooter's sister.

"Watching your career unfold," said Murray.

"I gather this means you want to sleep with me?" asked Biji.

"Hoooo," said the balding little starmaker.

"Will you let me shoot this commercial if I don't?" asked Biji.

"Sure," said Murray Feldman. "But nobody will ever see it."

"Ah," said Biji.

"I can make things happen for you, Biji Steinberg," said little Feldman.

"Is there a time limit on this proposal?" said Biji.

"Are you asking for time to decide?" asked Murray.

"No," said Biji. "I'm asking you if I have to sleep with you for a long time."

"Only as long as you want footlights and applause," said Murray Feldman.

Murray was being as clever and as frank as he knew how, but his libido was blinding him to things that he had seen earlier in Biji, things that would guarantee Biji's success with him or without him. The odd-eyed girl knew that she really didn't have a choice if she wanted to break into show business. Once in, she knew, she wouldn't need short Murray.

"I will sleep with you," said Biji, closing in on Murray, naked except for a half-zipped surfing jacket. "But it's going to cost you."

"I can afford it," said Murray, taking her arm and burying his nose in the moist inside of her elbow.

Biji watched him nuzzle her. "That's what you think," she said, moving to the roll of the boat.

Biji was at the age where girls with more normal aspirations and contacts make career decisions about college or professional training. Adam and Sharon

Steinberg were so delighted with Biji's modeling and acting successes that they said nothing to her about an education. If Adam Steinberg had even dreamed about the kind of education his daughter was receiving at the hands and lips of Murray Feldman, he would surely have turned ax murderer.

Sharon was less naive about the wiles of men than her husband, having made her way into the Bel Air community largely on her back. She was immediately suspicious of the nights that Biji spent away from home and grew rude and nosy when Biji announced that she was going to move out into her own apartment.

"How much money have you made?" asked Sharon.

"Ask Daddy," Biji replied. "He seems to keep quite an eye on that sort of thing."

"Not enough to afford your own place for very long," countered Sharon.

"She's made more than enough to afford to rent a place," said lawyer Adam the perfectionist, walking in upon the discussion.

Sharon shot him a furious look.

"It doesn't bother you that our daughter is moving out to an apartment at the age of eighteen?"

"I think it's wonderful," said Adam.

"Are you seeing any boys?" asked Sharon.

"You can't even imagine," Biji said.

"Watch you don't get pregnant," said Sharon.

"I'm always careful," Biji said.

Adam was already thinking about whom among his old friends or classmates he could call and brag to about Biji's success. He was also thinking about what he could do with her room. For Adam, Biji's burgeoning career was part of the natural course of things that he had planned for his child and his life. The name Adam Steinberg had gained significant heft in the years since Bernard's capture. Adam had even graduated from East Coast squash to West Coast tennis, and the law partner with whom he played was one of the first people he called. After telling the man about Biji's successes and setting up the afternoon's game, Adam Steinberg called his old Yale chum, Sharon's gynecologist, to give him the good news. The doctor had shared in so much family tragedy, Adam reasoned, it was time to shoot some glad tidings his way.

"She's moving out," said Adam.

"Is everything all right between you?" asked the doctor.

"Oh sure, sure," said Adam. "She's got a career going, you know. I guess budding Hollywood actresses don't live at home with their parents. It's good for me"—Adam dropped his voice—"I get to use the room for my bird drawings."

"Well, I think it's marvelous news," said the gynecologist.

"You haven't seen her in years, have you?" said Adam.

"No," said the doctor. "No, I haven't. She always seems to be out somewhere when you and I get together."

"She's a knockout," said Adam.

"Always was," said the doctor.

"Sharon's worried that if she gets her own place, she's going to screw around and get knocked up."

"Hmm," said the doctor.

"Should I worry about that?" Adam asked.

"I don't really think so," said the doctor.

"And what about diseases—herpes, the clap, AIDS?"

"AIDS could be a worry," said the gynecologist.

"I'm sure she uses some kind of birth control."

"Perhaps you should discuss this with her," said the baby doctor.

"What about if I have her call you?" asked Adam.

"I think it might be more appropriate if you talk to her yourself. You don't want her to get the impression you don't care."

"Nah. The kid's great. She knows how I feel about her."

"Whatever you think's best," said the doctor. "I'd love to see her."

"Biji!" Adam Steinberg yelled upon hanging up the telephone.

"Adam!" Biji yelled back from the kitchen, where she sat chopping eggplant with her mother.

"I hate it when you call your father by his first name," said Sharon.

"You don't think I know him well enough?" asked Biji.

"I want you to go see your mother's doctor," Adam said, appearing at the door by the refrigerator.

"Shit," said Biji.

"Nice talk," Adam observed.

"I just cut myself," said the eighteen-year-old actress, holding up a neatly sliced finger.

"I hope you didn't get any blood on the eggplant," said Sharon.

With Murray Feldman's help Biji found an apartment at the north end of Malibu Beach in a set of new town houses right by the water. Murray paid the rent, but Biji did all the decorating. The youngest Steinberg had a great love for Art Deco, which she got from the few pieces that her mother had around the house. In general, Sharon's tastes were poorly developed and unrefined, but she did have a good eye, and the Bel Air house featured a beautiful Art Deco mirror with black lacquer fringework and a nearly perfect colored-glass vase, which Biji had stolen for her room and kept filled, always with a single rose. These two items she took without asking her mother and bought others to match. Murray Feldman insisted upon moving in an undersized leather recliner, which he positioned right by the window with the best ocean view. Biji detested the chair, which had cigarette burns in it though Murray didn't smoke and which was too small for her to use herself without her feet hanging off into space.

"You're going to have to change your name," said Murray one night about half a year after Biji had moved to Malibu. He sat upright on the chair that Biji hated so much, his round white belly peeking out from a black velour housecoat.

"Want to tell me why?" said Biji, who knew damn well but wanted to hear Murray say it.

"Because you're not a star yet, and a French Jewish name isn't going to help your career any."

"What name would you suggest?" asked Biji.

"I'm glad you asked that question," said Murray, adjusting the telescope that stood on a tripod by his elbow so that he could look into the bedroom of the town house next door where a slightly overweight blond woman was undressing.

"You have a name in mind then?" said Biji.

"Now it's just her hairdresser and me who know for sure," muttered Murray, squinting through the lens.

"You have a name in mind then?" repeated Biji.

"I have more than a name," said the producer. "I have a new role."

"Oh?" said Biji, immediately all ears and schemes.

"I'm going to put you opposite Hollywood's most famous leading man."

"Go on," said Biji.

"He's black," said Murray Feldman with a smirk.

"I know that," said Biji Steinberg, who had rarely seen a black person, knew her parents were prejudiced, and felt that she should make a deliberate effort not to be.

"It's a story about a famous kidnapping."

"A true one?" said Biji.

"Come rub this for me," said Murray Feldman.

"I said is it a real kidnapping?" said Biji, moving to Murray's chair.

"It's loosely based on the banana-bantling case, you know, where they found the little baby on the docks at San Pedro?"

"Do I play a loving wife?" said Biji.

"The very role we are about to rehearse," said Murray with his certain grin.

Biji stretched her hands far above her head, wrists together, and knelt by the leather recliner with a sigh.

"What do you think of the name Lee Frisk?" asked Murray Feldman, struggling to right himself.

16

Confronted with Faranak, Scooter's virginity did not last long. The growing Loon flung himself into love with such abandon that even the sooty air of New Haven smelled like flowers. Classwork and home studies passed by like cotton dreams. After dating him for a month, the Persian girl moved into Scooter's little apartment, but she found no space for her forty pairs of shoes. Also, she complained bitterly that the warped windows let the draft in. In the end, in a rather unorthodox arrangement, Scooter gave his place to Faranak's roommate, a mousy girl named Tracy who wore glasses too narrow for her face. Scooter took Tracy's room in Faranak's two-bedroom undergraduate suite and put his clothing, his books, and his motorcycle tools there. He kept his alarm clock and his toothbrush in with Faranak, where he slept. Gothic eaves on the outside of the residential college provided refuge for his beloved Ducati, which lay dormant and stiff underneath a nylon cover when the days were too blustery.

One day Scooter came home from class early. There had been a guest lecture by a professor from the Russian department on Soviet economics and business organization. The professor, a small and elderly man with crusty lips, had brought black bread and sweet pickles with him and set them up on a side table along with seltzer. The students munched while they listened and Scooter was surprised to find that he enjoyed the talk and that it went quickly. When he returned too early to the dorm room, he found it deserted. All the undergraduates were still in class. The lecture had moved him into the Slavic mode, and he felt relaxed and warm. A perfect time, he decided, for a walk to the liquor store on the west side of the campus. Once there, he perused the crates and labels until he found a bottle of one-hundred-proof Russian vodka.

"Gonna tie one on?" asked the portly cashier with a grin.

"Don't know," he said, and he really didn't, since despite Roman's whoring and boozing, Scooter had never been truly drunk in his life.

"Why not try some Carlsberg Elephant as a chaser," said the man.

"What is it?"

"You've never heard of the Elephant?" said the cashier in mock horror.

"Wine?" asked Scooter Loon.

"Beer. It's beer. The strongest, deepest, richest beer in the world."

"You're the salesman," said Scooter with a smile. "I'll try it."

"Good choice"—the man grinned—"and on sale too."

When Scooter returned to Faranak's quarters with the vodka and the ale, she was still not home. He turned on the radio, leaned back in his beanbag chair, and looked at the gray sky. Sometime during his third beer a heavy snow began to fall.

Scooter did not know that the whole town, along with most of the Northeast, was about to be paralyzed by the heaviest snowfall in ten years. The TV and radio weathermen were even more surprised than Scooter when the snow got wetter and thicker and began to stick like resin. For a fleeting moment the eleven-fingered boy worried about his cherished Ducati, but his concern fled in the face of the Russian firewater, and he was halfway through the bottle before he realized he had never seen real snow before. He tried to stand up for a better look out the window, but he fell back down and began to giggle. At that moment the telephone rang.

"Yaylo," said Scooter, making a grab for it and ending up on his back with his feet in the air.

"Hey there, young fella," said Roman Loon on the transcontinental wire. "I hear you're having quite a storm back there."

"Alarm," said Scooter.

"I say you're having quite a snowstorm back there in Connecticut."

"Yep, snowing."

"Did I call at a bad time? You got your little Persian girl in the sack there or something?"

"Nimejeslyinhere," Scooter Loon told his father.

"What're you, drunk? Have you been drinking? Good boy! Marian," screamed Roman, "Scooter's been drinking! What're you drinkin'? I hope it's whiskey."

"Beer," Scooter managed.

"You got that drunk on beer? I hope you haven't wet your pants."

"Nionlihadthree."

"Three beers made it so you can't talk? What, you got frostbite on your tongue?" Roman laughed.

At this moment Scooter heard the door open and then a stamping of boots. Faranak appeared in the doorway wearing a black wool coat and a red scarf, snow flakes stuck to her thick black hair. She waved at Scooter, but he had trouble waving back because he was upside down.

"Nihadsomvodkatoo," Scooter mumbled into the phone.

Faranak walked in and sized up the situation in an instant.

"Who're you talking to?" she said, her coat still on.

"My father," said Scooter.

"What about your father?" said Roman Loon, feeling suddenly cold even though it was seventy-two degrees in Santa Barbara.

Faranak reached down and took the phone from Scooter's hand.

"Hello, Mr. Loon," she said in her husky voice. "This is Scooter's friend, Faranak. I'm afraid Scooter has had too much to drink."

"Are you the Persian girl?" said Roman.

"I am from Iran, yes."

"Scooter thinks the world of you."

"I think the world of Scooter, too, Mr. Loon. I am only sorry he is so drunk right now." While she talked Scooter was playing with her cold, wet shoes and running his hand, from below, up the inside of her leg.

"Oh, that's all right," said Roman. "Nothing wrong with a man taking a drink now and then, long as it doesn't get in the way of things, if you know what I mean."

"I think I do, Mr. Loon."

"I hear you're having a hell of a snow back there."

"It is beginning now, that is for sure," said Faranak.

"I won't keep you, sweetheart. You just take good care of my hard-drinking boy."

"I will take good care of him, Mr. Loon. Nice to talk to you."

Faranak hung up and took her coat, scarf, and hat off. Scooter was still upside down with his feet on the beanbag chair, watching her every move and sipping what was left of a full glass of straight vodka.

"Silly man," said Faranak. "You are dribbling your drink on your shirt."

"Snoproblem," said Scooter.

"Yes, there will be a problem with the snow," Faranak told him.

"I'm hungry," he said. "Iwanagoateat."

"We can't go out anywhere, silly man," said Faranak. "All the restaurants are closing. There's a big snow outside."

"I want falafel," said Scooter, sitting up with a big effort to appear sober. The malformed man had never had Mideastern cuisine until he had met Faranak, and now he was crazy for spicy things made with beans and pastes, like hummus, tahini, falafel, and baba ganouch.

"That place is going to be closed for sure," said Faranak.

"Callemup," said Scooter.

"That food will make you sick."

"Okay then," said Scooter. "I will call them."

While Faranak found the number for Achmed's Cafe, Scooter clawed his way upright against the windowsill and pushed at the glass.

"What are you doing?" she asked him, her fingers in the yellow pages.

"Nilefthevodkaoutthere," said Scooter, pointing to the narrow ledge outside the window. "Sgotabeecold."

Faranak retrieved the icy drink and called the restaurant.

"Gimmethephone," said Scooter, sticking out his hand. She handed it to him.

"Achmed's Cafe," said a voice on the other end of the line that sounded to Scooter remarkably like Faranak.

"Youpenfordinner?" asked Scooter Loon.

"We are open three hundred and eighty-five days a year."

"Thanks," said Scooter.

"No problem, my friend," said the man from Achmed's Cafe.

"We have to go there," said Scooter. "Stimeforfalefel."

Faranak put her black coat on again and wound her red scarf around her neck. She supported Scooter by the elbow while the famous racer dressed in his motorcycle boots and a leather jacket and sweater. The pair made their way out of the dormitory with Scooter humming loudly and Faranak feeling embarrassed. They trudged through the snow toward Achmed's and Scooter had to look at the ground so that the cold wind wouldn't go up his nose and make him gasp. Snow was sticking to his blue jeans.

"I have a question for you, Scooter Loon," said Faranak, skipping once to match her step with his.

"Mlistening," said Scooter, concentrating on his walking.

"What does your father do for his work?"

"Dosnmatter," said Scooter solemnly.

"Pardon me, please," said Faranak, who smelled like flowers.

"He runs a motorcycle shop," said Scooter, suddenly feeling sober.

When they arrived at Achmed's, Scooter ordered a plateful of mixed wild grains and lamb. Then he went to the men's room to wash his hands. Faranak sat and waited for him, his food came, and he did not return. When he had been gone nearly half an hour, she went to find him. She discovered the men's room at the bottom of a long steep flight of stairs. She knocked on the door and heard water running but no reply. She knocked again and entered.

Scooter Loon was standing in front of the basin staring at himself in the mirror. The drain was open and cold water was running over his hands, making them shriveled like an old man's. Faranak watched as he massaged each hand with the other, over and over, under the stream.

"It's time to go home, silly man," said Faranak, taking his arm.

"The truth is," said Scooter Loon, looking up the long stair-case, "he's a burglar."

17

The chameleon in Biji Steinberg allowed her to physically and emotionally shift roles as easily as most people change underwear. There were, however, facets and shades of the acting profession that could be appreciated only through experience. On-camera etiquette, director's slang, and the finer points of committing dialogue to memory were all aspects of her trade that Biji needed to develop. Murray Feldman's gonads did lead him around by the nose, but not down a path that would lead to widespread ridicule and ruin. He knew that before Biji could star in a major motion picture, she would need a chance to grow. As a result Murray inserted her in a series of commercials and bit parts guaranteed to gain her maximum camera hours in the shortest possible time. Biji's schedule was frantic, and most of her evenings were devoted to tending to Murray's appetites. What upset the budding star most about this routine was that it didn't allow her to work out.

Jewish people are bent more to general education than exercise, but Biji was an exception. She had a strong need to test her system and sweat. Perhaps hormonal, this need could not be denied. If she sat still too long, the endorphins left her system and Biji became impossible.

Adam's squash games bore the Olympic standard for Biji's parents, but they had passed along fine coordination and stamina to both children. Scooter had what it took to win at high-speed motorcycle racing, and Biji had the body of a goddess with the frame and strength to match. Her well-formed and potent organs spoke to her through an urgent need; in order to feel good, she had to sweat. In her early years Biji would run around and around the block as if tethered to the Bel Air house like a yo-yo.

"I need to slow the pace a bit," Biji told the producer from across the dinner table at the Malibu apartment.

Murray took a bite of the halibut in white wine and mushrooms that Biji had prepared from Sharon's recipe.

"Can't slow down, girl. You need the practice if you want to be in the kidnapping picture."

"I just need an hour and a half a day to get some exercise. My body is falling apart."

"Not from where I'm sitting."

"I'm losing tone and flexibility," said Biji. "I don't feel strong. I get winded going up stairs."

"I'm going to get you winded now," said Murray, pushing his plate aside.

"You're being a shit," said Biji Steinberg. "I'm voicing a need to you. Are you going to pay attention or not?"

"Why not go to a gym?" the little producer suggested.

"A gym? You mean like a health club?"

"Sure. Row, bike, swim, use the Nautilus machines."

"Do you know a good one?" asked Biji.

Biji asked Murray for the name of a club just to be certain she didn't go there. She knew that an ogling by Murray's cronies was the last thing in the world she needed. After asking around some, she found a small gymnasium in West Los Angeles that was miles from where she did her shoots and far away from anyone she knew. The place she chose was not a meat market where men with big biceps went to bulge and sweet-talk women. It was a serious outfit, without a Jacuzzi or showers, known for the dedication and small size of the clientele and for the excellence of its trainers. When Biji signed up it was with a stout woman with very black hair and a pronounced mustache. Her name was Rosa.

"I'm not sure about you, girlie," Rosa said, shaking her head. "I'm not sure at all."

"I'm here to work out," said Biji, planting her hands on her hips.

"Maybe yes and maybe no," said Rosa. "But all's I know is that you are some looker, and we don't want no hanky-panky stuff going on in here."

"Forget that," said Biji, peeling to her leotard. "Make me sweat."

Rosa pursed her lips at Biji's perfect body.

"What exactly do you want from this place?" she asked.

"I want to get strong," said Biji Steinberg. "I want to feel good."

"I can make you strong," said Rosa. "The rest is up to you."

Biji inherited from her father an ability that she shared with Scooter Loon—namely, the capacity to concentrate utterly on something without letting a single stray thought cross her mind. She found weight lifting a perfect outlet. She began working on her upper body, trying to eliminate every last ounce of softness and flab. At the beginning she added bulk by using the Nautilus and Universal machines, pumping iron straight up from her chest and out from full extension to the sides inward, like a flapping bird. After several months of this, she progressed to so-called free weights. Her morning routine consisted of manipulating disks of iron strung across a barbell in the most contorted of positions. Lying on a bench, she brought her arms up over her head and then behind her, returning them with thirty or forty pounds to a position straight in front of her belly. She grunted and strained at pushes and pulls, the veins in her neck and legs forced to the surface, her muscles bunching under her taut moist skin. She dipped and twisted, too, always winding down a hard morning's workout with half an hour of stretching so that her movements would remain feminine and fluid. After half a year, Biji's body looked different, and Murray was concerned.

"Listen, Lee," he began, insisting on her stage name so that she would grow comfortable with it, "I'm telling you as a pro that you have to quit this stuff. Nobody wants a leading lady who looks like Hercules."

"You're exaggerating as usual," said Biji. "I don't look much different. And besides, if I do build up my body, maybe we can change people's tastes a little."

"Never enter into a relationship thinking you are going to change someone," said Murray.

"What you're saying is that I have to be the way people want me to be."

"If you want to be a star," said Murray Feldman, a man who had made many.

"I think I can have a strong body and still act well and look good," said Biji.

"Sweetheart, Lee, darling," said Feldman. "Your legs look like a runner's. Your arms are bigger than mine. Your stomach has ripples in it."

"You sound like you're afraid I'll beat you up," said Biji.

"I'm afraid you'll eat me alive," muttered Murray. "I'm afraid you'll draw me so far in, I won't be able to get out."

"Sounds like maybe you need to find a different part for me," said Biji.

Biji's morning workouts continued through her nineteenth birthday, when Murray announced that the kidnapping picture was finally taking real shape and that within a month Biji was going to have to get used to working in the mornings instead of pumping iron. Biji responded by switching her workout to late afternoon.

"I hate working out so late in the day," she told her trainer.

"Most of the girls like it because there are so many men," said Rosa, who had gained great respect for the quality of Biji's efforts and no longer thought of her as a flirt.

"I will admit to one thing," said Biji, straining to pull a pulley weight from above her shoulder down to her waist. "That guy over there is making me weak."

"No surprise," said the mustached lady. "He makes everybody weak."

"You too?" ribbed Biji with a gasp of effort.

"I am not a teenage girl at the movies," said Rosa.

"I don't get you," Biji said with a long sigh, replacing the chrome bar on its resting post.

"You know the face, don't you?"

"I guess I don't," Biji replied.

"Does the name Reno Raven mean anything to you?" said Rosa, cupping the front of Biji's ribs with her fat hand.

"Muh," said Biji, bending over to retie a shoelace and trying to think very fast. "It doesn't look like him."

"I have never seen him in a movie," said Rosa, " 'cause I don't go to movies."

"I want you to introduce me," she said, straightening.

"That's what they all say," said Rosa.

"Come on, Rosa, please."

"Go and introduce yourself. Girl looks like you, she don't need my help."

At that moment Reno Raven happened to finish his set of bench presses, swing his thick legs to the side, and sit up.

"I can't believe he works out here," said Biji. "You would think someone that famous would have a home gym."

"He's been working out here since he was a nobody," Rosa said. "Everyone knows not to bug him."

"He's looking at us," said Biji.

"He's looking at you," Rosa replied.

"Give me Reno or give me death," cried Biji, smiting herself on her firm breast. Rosa laughed.

Reno Raven had been watching Biji Steinberg for well over an hour. He had watched her from a supine position with two hundred pounds hovering over his face, and he had watched her while squatting, his quadriceps bulging and a constipated look on his face. All the watching had accomplished so far was to make him ache deep down and make concentration a chore. He thought she might be the most elegant girl he'd ever seen in his life.

Reno Raven was gigantic. He had always been gigantic. His mother joked that when his father harpooned her, she should have started stretching exercises right away. Reno stood six and a half feet tall, and at the gym wore spandex pants through which even his veins could be seen, especially if he was angry. From the neck down he looked like a Mr. Universe competitor, which he had in fact been, but from the neck up he

looked like a Roman senator. The most notable thing about
Reno Raven, however, was not his size, his good looks, or the
fact that he was the hottest ticket in Hollywood. The most
notable thing was his sense of humor. Just when the audience
thought Reno was about to break a man in half, he would say
something so funny that even teenagers in the back row, who
should have been busy kissing, would punch each other in the
arm and cackle.

When Reno rose from the Universal weight machine and
began to close on Biji and her trainer with giant strides, neither woman could do anything but stare. His lips were closed
tight, and he didn't look happy.

"I think he's going to knock our heads together," Biji said
in tiny tones.

"I told you he was looking at you," said Rosa.

"Give me Reno or give me death?" said Reno Raven. "I
gather you're my biggest fan?"

Biji shook her head. "Actually, I didn't even recognize
you," Biji replied. "I was just joking around with Rosa."

Reno Raven was used to ardent, fawning women chasing
him everywhere. One of the greatest battles of Reno's recent
life had been his struggle to keep his private life private. Like
all actors, however, Reno secretly reveled in the attention, and
it was with a measure of hurt that he received Biji's comment.

"But you have heard of me?"

"Oh, of course," said Biji. "But I've never seen one of your
movies."

"I gotta go," interrupted Rosa. "I have a blind yoga class to
run."

"Can you, in your wildest dreams, imagine Rosa doing
yoga?" said Reno, watching the bearded lady disappear into
the distance.

"No," said Biji, "and I think that's why she only teaches the
blind."

"Beautiful and witty too," said Reno Raven. "Have some
carrot juice with me?"

"If you'll tell me about your next movie," said Biji Steinberg, grabbing her towel.

"If you promise to keep it quiet," said Reno, swelling with the same satisfaction he always felt when he knew that he was over the hump with a woman.

"I'm very good at secrets," said Biji Steinberg.

"My next film's about the banana-bantling kidnapping case."

"How can they make a movie out of that?" asked Biji. "It hasn't been solved."

"Never will be, either," said Reno. "You can't ask a seven-month-old infant to pick his kidnapper out of a lineup."

"This is all very interesting," Biji said as they left the gym together, "but what I really want to hear about is your leading lady."

"I haven't met her yet," said Reno, "but I hear she's a knockout."

"You've never seen her in another movie?"

"She is," said Reno, opening the door to his waiting snow-white limo, "an unknown, a starlet new to the scene."

"She's probably screwing some producer," said Biji, ducking into the moving juice bar.

18

Scooter Loon's casual, almost disinterested manner of staying at the top of his business school class fused his more competitive classmates into a slow burn. He seemed to watch the blackboard with his eyes unfocused, and his name often had to be called twice during professorial inquisitions. Other men thought him childishly preoccupied with his motorcycle and resented the way he parked it in the corridor outside the study halls as if it were a dog awaiting his whistling summons. Women in his lectures found him unbearably attractive, not only for his fine physique, but for his total lack of bookishness. Picaresque rumors abounded, but nobody knew the real Scooter Loon.

His second year at graduate school, a time during which Faranak assumed Scooter would outgrow his Ducati and begin to talk seriously about the continuation of their relationship when he finished his graduate degree, found Scooter in a fettle.

"I learned a word for you today," said Faranak from deep within her woolen coat as they walked together to the library.

"Well?" said Scooter Loon.

"Churlish."

"I'm not sure what that means," he said.

"It means you can't be moved or changed, that you are untractable," said Faranak with her hypnotic Persian lilt.

"Intractable," said Scooter. "The word is *intractable,* not *untractable.*"

"You see?" said Faranak, locking her arm in his.

"I don't know what you're talking about."

"Why are you taking your motorcycle to class all of a sudden?" she asked.

"I don't like walking in the snow."

"Nobody likes walking in the snow, silly man. But to ride is so dangerous."

"I know what I'm doing," said Scooter.

"I look at your racing trophies and I am sure that you do," said Faranak. "But I watch your black tires spinning dirty snow onto your pants and then I do not know."

"You're just sore because I haven't taken you riding," said Scooter.

"I don't like riding on the back of a machine with dirt on my legs and the wind coming in the holes around my neck, that is for sure. I would like to go to the beach with you sometime, maybe in April."

"I've told you before that you can't go on a bike with one seat," said Scooter Loon.

"Then why do you have such a bike, a stubborn antisocial thing like that?"

"I didn't choose it," said Scooter Loon. "My father gave it to me."

"Something is happening to you," said Faranak. "That is for sure."

Persian women certainly have no less female intuition than women from other cultures, and it could be argued by some that they have more. In any case, Faranak paid deep attention to every line on Scooter's face and every pause in each of his rare sentences. She knew something was amiss and was as determined to uproot the thing as a hog after truffles.

"I had a call from my father," said Scooter.

"How nice," said Faranak.

"It wasn't a good call," said Scooter.

"When was this?"

"Two weeks ago Thursday."

"He is angry with you for not coming there for Christmas?"

"Disappointed, not angry. He waited until after we got back from skiing to give me the news."

"What news?" Faranak asked him as they entered the old stone dorm and the bright blue stairs where students just out of high school still spilled spit.

Scooter trudged up the steps and paid no attention.

"What news?" Faranak shouted up the staircase until the wet walls rang.

"My mother is dying," Scooter Loon called down the stairs.

Strong ethnic groups such as Muslims, Italians, and Jews tend to have more of a sense of family than the average American. When Faranak heard that the mother of the man she lived with was coming for a visit, she could think of nothing but how to please and honor her.

"Scooter Loon, this is wonderful news! We will make room for her! Don't even think of a hotel. Maybe even Tracy will let you take the old room back while your mother is here so that your mother can have a place that was yours. Oh, I have looked forward so much to meeting your mother. To have such patience with a boy who goes so fast!"

In all the time that she had known him, Faranak had never seen Scooter get physically angry. She had even heard the expression "cool as a cucumber" from one of her friends, and though she didn't understand the vegetable reference, she thought there was a ring about it that fit her Loon well.

When she got to the top of the stairs, Scooter was standing by the door to their room with a terrifying look in his eye. He was breathing fast and hard, and his hands shot out quickly until they gripped the fragrant girl around the neck.

"SHE'S NOT COMING FOR A VISIT!" screamed Scooter Loon. "SHE'S ON HER WAY OUT FROM THIS PLANET. SHE'S GOING TO BE DEAD!"

Scooter's unexpected violence, combined with the words he uttered, were too much for Faranak, who passed into unconsciousness also because Scooter's hands were not allowing any oxygen to get to her brain. As she slumped Scooter caught her and dragged her through the door, his breath coming in great heaves and gasps. He caressed her hair and stroked her forehead until she revived, and then they held each other and rocked and rocked.

Spring break comes late to Yale students but leaves a short pull until the summer. Scooter flew back to Santa Barbara the day before the intersession actually began and was met at the airport by Roman in the familiar turbocharged pickup truck. In the back was a striking yellow motorcycle, slender and with a single pair of white instruments. The vehicle was held in place by strong black nylon cords with plastic-coated hooks, the front wheel compressed and tense enough to leap catlike from the bed at a moment's unbinding.

"You look well, boy," said Roman, giving his son a hug and steering him by the shoulders to the side of the waiting motor.

"How's Mom?" Scooter said, returning the embrace and then throwing his bags into the back by the yellow bike.

"Waiting to see you, just waiting to see you is all. She's visiting with the neighbors, so we have time for a ride."

"She's visiting with the neighbors?" said Scooter. "What neighbors?"

"Some people she's been spending time with since you've been away, the sort of people that help you through this kind of thing."

"Doctors?" asked Scooter as Roman charged away from the curb at the tiny airport.

"Not doctors, not really," said Roman, anxious to avoid the subject of the hospice crew.

"Nurses?"

"Not nurses either. Say, how about a little ride up San Marcos Pass? I brought the yellow beauty there, and she's just waiting for your touch."

"I want to see Mother. We can ride later," said Scooter.

"I told her that we would be taking a ride together, you see, and I don't think she minds."

"Forget the ride! I want to see my mother," Scooter yelled at the man who long ago had stolen him from underneath the noses of the slumbering Steinbergs.

Roman Loon slammed on the brakes and turned to Scooter, grabbing him the same way his son had grabbed Faranak weeks before.

"There are some things," roared Roman Loon, sounding remarkably like a true British cat burglar, "that just don't

change no matter what happens. Now I say we go for a ride."
With this he put the truck in gear again and headed for Loon
Motors, where his Laverda triple lay warm and waiting.

Scooter watched his father carefully as the older man un-
loaded the yellow bike from the bed of the truck, easing it
down an aluminum ramp that flexed slightly with the weight.
He had said nothing since the attack, understanding suddenly
that his father was coping the only way he knew how.

"She's a Yamaha single," said Roman.

"A Jap bike?" said Scooter. "I don't believe it!"

"I've done a little work on her," Roman said. "Wait'll you
ride her."

"Now where have I heard that before," said Scooter, allowing himself the first smile of the day.

The pair rode up the freeway from Loon Motors and onto
the entrance to winding Highway 154. Scooter could barely
hear the thrum of the triple over the drill of the Yamaha. The
little bike was far lighter and smaller than his familiar Ducati,
but it pulled under the throttle like an air force fighter. He
banked through the corners gently, getting the feel of the bike,
following his father's steady lead. When the road straightened
to surmount a small gully, Scooter opened the little Yamaha
up until the engine felt like it was going to shake from the
frame. The road shrank before him until it was only as wide as
pencil lead and the speedometer was pegged at 135. With the
wind drowning his thoughts and the engine shaking his atoms,
Scooter Loon was as calm as when he floated in the fluid of
Sharon Steinberg. Then he followed Roman to visit Marian at
the home for the hopeless.

Marian Loon, in the eight
months since Scooter had seen her last, had shrunken to a
skeleton. Her hair, the same dead protein that had draped over
Scooter and tickled him in a dark curtain years before, was
missing in most places and thin where it remained. Her starving skin no longer had the luxury of wrinkling, since it was

doing all it could to simply cover her tiny body and so was as smooth as a child's.

"I turn the trouble of my incontinence merely upon myself," said Scooter Loon, kneeling to her and pressing her bony hand to his cheek.

Even in her darkest hour Marian Loon still had a beautiful smile.

"Vexed I am, with passions of some difference, conceptions proper only to myself . . ." She grinned.

". . . which give some soil to my behaviors," Scooter finished.

"It's her pancreas," said Roman, standing behind her and pushing the rocker in which she sat forward and back.

"Oh, Roman," said Marian Loon. "Always talking in such technical terms."

"He's a mechanic, Mother," said Scooter, "he can't help it."

"Now he's a mechanic," she said. "Yes, now. And how is your pretty Persian girl?"

"How do you know she's pretty?" asked Scooter.

"Your mother's been writing to her," Roman interrupted. "She sent us a picture."

"She sent you a picture?"

"She's very pretty in the picture," said Marian. "Such uncomplicated skin, so smooth and brown."

"She wanted to come with me," said Scooter, "but we couldn't afford it."

"That's not the way she tells it," said Roman. "She says you wouldn't let her."

"I just didn't want . . ." said Scooter, looking deep into Marian's eyes. "I just didn't want to share you right now."

Roman Loon made a choking sound behind the chair.

"You know what I think," said Marian Loon, her eyes suddenly bright and wet. "I think you two should go for a ride."

"We've just been for a ride."

"You have?"

"Dad insisted."

"Did you see his new motorcycle?"

"A Japanese bike," said Scooter. "I couldn't believe my eyes."

"But with a new engine," said Roman.

"I wish I could have a new engine," said Marian.

Roman ran from the room.

19

Because her different-colored eyes not only let in light and motion but were connected to a sharp brain, nineteen-year-old Biji Steinberg had a good understanding of how to get ahead in Hollywood. She knew that budding starlets were as common as green leaves and that to stand out she had to be identified with a power person. The first such force in her life had been her father, the second was Murray Feldman. Now she was ready to bask in the aura of Reno Raven. The transition was to come swiftly, for where Reno went, his public followed.

One night, after a quiet dinner in a posh Polish restaurant near the gym in West Los Angeles, Reno and Biji emerged into the alley where the black man's white limo waited patiently with glowing lights. The actor was wearing a pair of loose-fitting black trousers gathered at the waist and a red button-down shirt open deep to reveal his hard chest. Biji wore jeans, a wide belt, and a silk blouse. These duds were significant because they were to be seen, in full and glorious color, all over the cover of *Star Life* magazine the following week.

The alley offered a number of hiding spots, and the two gossip reporters took advantage of them. One hid in a Dumpster, the long lens of his camera protruding from beneath the heavy metal lid. He used extremely grainy, high-speed film, which yielded a photographic record, if not a quality image, of Biji Steinberg and Reno Raven walking arm in arm. The other reporter, a ballsier sort, crouched behind Reno's limousine, unseen by its driver.

"Some borscht," said Reno as the kitchen door closed behind him. Reno usually opted for the back way out so that he could maintain some modicum of privacy.

"I liked my trout with dill," said Biji. "but your rabbit surprised me. I thought you were veggie."

"With these tree-trunk forearms," said Raven, "I need all the protein I can get."

"Fish and soy protein is just as good," Biji said. "In fact, kidney beans and limas—"

At that moment there was a great flashing and scraping, and the *Star Life* reporters emerged to record the moment forever on film.

"No!" Reno roared, tackling the man who had crouched by his car in an almost insane desire to protect his right to privacy.

Biji could hear the high-pitched recycling of the flash unit as the man's camera hit the ground. Reno Raven's chauffeur leapt from the front seat and looked about, spying at once the offending lens and the trash bin ajar. He heaved the metal lid and withdrew the reporter with a heave so quick that the lid fell closed on air.

In all fairness, the two photographers, although new to the Raven tail, had been warned of his proclivity for violence when his privacy was threatened. They had laughed only hours earlier about these rumors, agreeing that Hollywood loves excess and doubting that any real harm could come of a few photos.

Reno's chauffeur was also his weight-training partner, though Biji had not seen them work out together. He was a big man, at least as big as his boss, but with far coarser features and little flair. He lowered the high-speed film man to the ground with one uncurling bicep and sat on his belly, his calves sandwiching the man's head. Then he lit a cigarette.

In the meantime Reno had his man's jawbone grinding the asphalt, his arm twisted up behind him in what seemed to Biji an impossible angle. Though the young actress had seen plenty of violence in films, she had never seen blood spilled on the street, and it filled her with the same numbness that overcame her brother at the La Carrera goat crash.

"Stop!" she shouted, running to Reno and trying to pull him off his victim by yanking on his massive shoulders. The photographer gurgled beneath Reno, his neck arched so that he could get a look at his guardian angel. "Let them up!"

When boiling-mad Reno caught a glimpse of Biji's expression, he relaxed slowly and let the reporter up off the ground.

"This is asinine," she said. "They're just doing their stupid job trying to get pictures of you for the paper." The chauffeur had followed Reno's lead and had released his man as well. "Let me talk to them in the car!"

The *Star Life* staffers looked at each other with wild eyes and then shrugged. Reno's man wiped his chin. Biji brought them together and drew them after her into the spacious backseat of the limo with its barful of carrot juice and lime. Reno and his driver stood outside, chests still heaving slightly as Biji closed the door with a thunk.

"I'm sorry," she said to the two men, keeping a warm hand on each one's knee. "He's a very private person, and he hates it when guys like you get sneaky."

"If he's so private, he shouldn't be an actor," the photographer with the bloody jaw muttered, holding his chin.

"Maybe not," said Biji, "but he is and he's a damn good one."

"Who are you anyway?" said the second man, wiping tomato and old french fries off of his clothes from his stint in the Dumpster.

"You smell terrible," said Biji Steinberg.

"Are you going to tell us who you are," said the first photographer, "or are you going to turn us back over to the goon squad and let us die here, beaten and curious?"

"I'll tell you anything you want to know," said Biji sweetly, "but since I've done you a little favor, maybe you can do me one too."

In the end the photographers agreed to omit mention of the fight with Raven in return for an exclusive on Biji and her relationship with the famous man. Biji promised to deliver some good pictures of herself to their office the next day, and by the time they emerged from the limo, Reno's temper had cooled.

The following week *Star Life* came out with the issue that would truly launch Biji's career. The headline read "Starlet Lectures Well-known Rabbit Eater on the Perils of Red Meat." The front cover of the tabloid showed Biji Steinberg in the same wet-suit top that she had worn for the toothpaste commercial near the port where the banana bantling was recovered. It was a picture she had taken from a silver frame in her apartment, a picture Murray Feldman treasured dearly and kept with him in miniature in his wallet. Beneath the large color blowup of Biji's tight thighs was a black-and-white picture of Reno Raven smiling broadly and with his arm around Biji. The article called Biji Steinberg "Lee Frisk," and talked about her upcoming role opposite Reno in the film version of the miraculous kidnapping and recovery of the banana bantling.

When Reno Raven saw the article he realized that his new girlfriend Biji Steinberg was the same as his future costar Lee Frisk and he knew that he'd been duped. At the same time he marveled at Biji's nerve, and his famous sense of humor took over.

"All this time"—he shook his head with a smile—"all this time you knew all about the movie and you would ask me just so that you could laugh at me inside."

"Not so," Biji insisted stubbornly. "I had to know about your attitude toward Lee Frisk. It was a professional issue. I wanted to get to know you better, that's all."

"You've got some balls," said Raven. "Sweet Jesus, I never saw such balls as yours."

"Except your own." Biji smiled.

"I should strangle your ass," said Raven.

"Isn't there something you'd rather do?"

"Oh baby, oh momma, how she pulls my strings." Reno Raven rolled his eyes and grabbed for the lanky, auburn-haired girl.

When Murray Feldman received his copy of *Star Life* he rushed to Biji's apartment with drool covering his left cheek.

"You're two-timing me with a *schwartze*?" cried little Murray, raising the magazine and slapping it down on his thigh over and over again.

"What?" said Biji.

"You're two-timing me with a miserable *schwartze*?"

"If you're referring to Reno in some Yiddish slang that I'm supposed to understand," began Biji, "you can just forget that stuff. After all, you put me opposite him in the banana-bantling movie—"

"There's not going to be any goddamn bantling movie," Murray Feldman raged. "I'm canceling it right now. No movie, no part for you, no nothing."

Little men are used to making whales out of carp, and Murray Feldman was no exception. Biji knew that he was first and last a film director and that first and last he loved himself.

"Don't be a jerk, Murray," she told him. "You can't just cancel a twenty-million-dollar film because you caught me sleeping with the star."

"And now you flaunt it in my face," he screamed, his hairless head showing bulging veins. "Now you admit that you've had sex with that jungle man! I'll see to it that you never work again. I'm going to call your parents right now."

At this Biji blanched, but it was too late. Murray sat on the arm of his beloved leather recliner and dialed the house of Adam and Sharon Steinberg.

"Adam? This is—"

At this Biji ran to the phone and tried to rip it from his grasp.

"It's Biji," she yelled. "Don't believe anything he says!"

"Adam this is Murray Feldman," the producer panted into the phone. "Biji needs you right now, she's in trouble, come quick." Murray yelled the address into the phone and hung up with Biji still trying to pry his fingers from the line.

When lawyer Adam and Sharon, his wife, arrived at the Malibu apartment where the famous producer Murray Feldman kept their daughter as his mistress, they found Biji tied atop the coffee table, her ankles secured by nylons to two table legs, her wrists by suspenders to two others. She was wearing nothing else.

"Come in, by all means come in," Murray Feldman said nasally, with a genial sweep of his hand. "I just want to talk to you about your daughter."

"Don't listen to him," said Biji sullenly, tugging at her bonds.

"What the hell's going on here?" said Adam, who suddenly understood and tried to keep from staring at the perfect and voluptuous body of his daughter.

"He's been keeping me here to play his skin flute," said Biji from near the ground.

"For heaven's sake," said Sharon, reaching to Biji's knots.

"I think you've carried this a little far, Murray," said Adam Steinberg the perfectionist, who nearly a quarter of a century earlier hadn't wanted his maimed infant son returned.

"You think so," Murray said, his voice shrill. "Then look at this. She's been making it with a *schwartze*."

"A *schwartze*?" said Sharon.

"Look at the picture."

"Yeah, but what a *schwartze*," said Sharon, ceasing her efforts to free Biji and peeking at the magazine over Adam's shoulder.

"Will somebody please untie me?" said Biji.

"You have to be careful who you sleep with," said Sharon, looking sternly at her daughter. "You might get pregnant."

"Don't you care that this man has kept me here as his mistress?" asked Biji, turning nearly over on one side.

"Well, we sort of suspected," said Adam.

"Actually we knew," Sharon admitted. "I mean a couple of toothpaste commercials do not a Malibu address achieve."

"Will somebody please untie me?" Biji screamed at last.

"You might have gotten pregnant," said Sharon with a sigh, cutting Biji's ropes with Adam's pocketknife.

"I CAN'T GET PREGNANT," Biji yelled again. "I'M ALL CUT UP INSIDE."

There were several moments of silence as Biji stood up and covered herself with a cushion from the sofa. She was breathing loudly.

Murray Feldman was the first to speak. "What're you talking about?" he asked.

"God are you lame, Murray." Biji rolled her eyes. "I mean I had an abortion by mommy's doctor and he cut me up so I can't ever have kids again."

Sharon Steinberg turned white and fell to the floor.

"Did the doctor tell you this?" asked Adam.

"He didn't have to," Biji said, her voice getting smaller and smaller until she, too, sank down. "There are certain things a woman just knows."

"She's barren and sleeping with a *schwartze*," said Murray Feldman.

Adam knelt by Sharon and started to slap her face gently.

"Are you going to marry this Raven?" he said, not looking at his daughter.

All of a sudden Murray Feldman started to laugh. At first it was a low chuckle, but it grew and grew until he was positively shaking, his little belly quivering like raw filet on a toothpick.

"Good God," he said to Adam between gasps for air. "Listening to you, I think I know why she's the way she is."

20

Scooter Loon's two years at Yale's School of Organization and Management offered a reprieve from his career crisis. School obstacles fell easily before him, academic trials were mere irritations, and scholarships and awards abounded. As long as he was applying himself to a specific task, Scooter felt that he didn't have to worry about the long run. The end of the degree program, however, coupled with his mother's grave illness, brought all of Scooter's old problems back again. He was too good at too many things and had too many options. He could, he realized as he sat on the edge of his bed in Faranak's dorm room holding his diploma, be or do just about anything he pleased. If he wanted a job in business, recruiters bearing six-figure starting salaries were waiting. If he wanted to race motorcycles professionally, he had no doubt that he could do that, too, perhaps with worldwide success. Yet young Loon was as uninterested in the ivory parchment in his hand as he was in making love to his beautiful Persian girlfriend. He was devoid of all forward motion, and even with Faranak's support he sleepwalked through his final months at Yale, foundering amid his own dreams and ambitions, feeling very, very sorry for himself.

The Connecticut summer came late and heavy. The nearby ocean pushed air with a characteristic Atlantic smell in over the coast and the days were balmy. Scooter spent the weeks after his graduation hobnobbing with the summer graduate-student community by night and riding about on his Ducati by day. Having received her undergraduate degree at the same time that Scooter received his master's, Faranak had elected to stay the summer in New Haven instead of returning to Iran. Scooter knew she was waiting for something to happen between them, and as much as he wanted to return to his mother's bedside, he thought he should stay East until he knew what he was going to do.

"You already have a plan, I suppose," said Scooter, leaning against Faranak's fine furniture and drinking a beer.

"I have accepted an investment-bank training program in New York," she said.

"When did you do that?" he said, putting the bottle down.

"I did it today. One of us had to make a move. Now you can come to New York with me."

"I have to go back to California," said Scooter.

"For a time I think so," said Faranak, "and I shall go with you. But after . . ."

"After what?" said Scooter, with a provocative intensity that was becoming more and more typical.

Faranak just looked at him sadly. "It will do you good to be in New York," she said softly. "There are so many opportunities for a brilliant person like you. You never even know what you will do in the end."

"Everyone knows what they will do in the end," said Scooter Loon. "In the end they lie down and die."

"This kind of talk is not like you," said Faranak. "I'm so sorry about your mother."

"I'm going to take a week away," said Scooter. "I'm going to take what's left of my student loan and ride my bike to Maine."

Faranak clapped her hands in front of her full figure and positively bounced for joy.

"That is a wonderful idea, Scooter Loon," she said. "I have wanted to go so much to see the whale houses."

"Whaling houses," said Scooter. "Whale houses means where whales live. Anyway, I'm going alone, by myself, on the Ducati."

"You will take this trip without me?" said Faranak.

"You know there is only room for one," said Scooter.

"We could take my car," Faranak said, rubbing up against the Loon so that he could smell the toilet water that had snared him once.

"I'm sorry," he said. "I have to go alone."

"Of course," she said at once, drawing back from him and standing as tall as her petite spine would allow. "You must go and clear your mind. When you come back we will find you a job in the big pineapple."

Scooter's motorcycling nose drew him straight for the twisting road that lined the flatlands of the coast first seen by the Pilgrims on their way to Plymouth Rock. He left New Haven early one morning and motored as gently as his race bike would allow into the yellow glow of the rising sun. He had laden the Ducati's tailpiece with a sleeping bag and some clothes tied together with bungee cords. When he stopped for an occasional traffic light, Scooter smelled mussels and heard the sounds of many tourists with big cars, balloons, and colas.

The Ducati's crouched-over riding position made freeway cruising uncomfortable, but to make time on his way north Scooter left the twisting coastal roads for stints on the four-lane. He made it through Connecticut, Massachusetts, and New Hampshire the first day and slept in a state park, awakening under a pine tree to the dew and a spider on his cheek. The adventure really began the second day as he veered east and then west, east and then west, leaning his machine through pastoral turns, watching for cow dung and thinking of Marian.

Coastal Maine is characterized by hundreds, perhaps thousands, of tiny rocky inlets and bays. The littoral area is rich in kelp beds, and the water is so cold that oxygen is trapped between molecules of the sea, supporting myriads of tiny organisms. These planktonic forms support other, larger forms, and in the end anchor the food chain for marine mammals. Scooter had a fascination with dolphins and whales, stemming from childhood readings about their interactions with young Greek boys and bolstered by university articles about their formidable intelligence. At every juncture where the sea came in tight to the road, Scooter would park his bike on the pebbly shoulder and stare out over the water in hopes of a fin or spout. Often he mistook a bulb of kelp for a cetacean, and his heart would leap and he would watch and watch until he realized that the movement was random and due only to the tides. Other times he would think that the upended tail of a seabird was something more interesting, until the bird emerged, scanned the shore briefly, seeming to lock eyes with Loon, and took off.

The second day Scooter stopped in Freeport, Maine, to look at the famous camping and supply store there. He chose a prominent place next to the store sign and left his belongings strapped to the machine. Inside, he was bedazzled by the array of outdoor gear. He found oiled-wool fishing sweaters from Ireland and special pocketknives that opened to forks and scissors and tiny picks. He had never seen so much refined equipment for the sportsman. Neither Santa Barbara nor New Haven had such a store, and despite that fact that he was relatively free of material addictions, Scooter found himself wanting many things. He liked a certain rain slicker, for example, that was thick and orange and had big pockets that sealed with bright yellow Velcro. He had no protection from the rain, and he knew that he was tempting fate by riding the old seacoast road during a season notorious for storms. He also developed an attachment for a small rucksack made from leather, which looked as if it would fit snugly and comfortably against his back while he rode. He fondled the soft glove leather and a salesman caught his eye and nodded knowingly.

Perhaps it was something in the man's look that brought Bernard Steinberg's hand around to pat the pocket of his blue jeans and check for his wallet. Perhaps, too, he was thinking about purchasing the slicker or the pack, even though he knew he could afford neither. Whatever the root of the urge, it was a timely one, for when his hand went to his billfold it was not there.

Scooter's panic was completely out of character and stemmed from more than just worry that he would not be able to pay for gas back to New Haven. The loss of his wallet seemed to signify the general state of disarray that characterized his life. He was angry that he couldn't afford the slicker or the sack, and felt a sudden, intense need for a livelihood and cash. He grew very pale.

"Is there something wrong?" asked the salesman, a college boy who wore an alligator shirt and had Scooter's eye for finery but not his self-discipline. The boy sized up Scooter's windblown hair and creased leather jacket. He looked at his faded jeans and his motorcycle boots.

"My wallet," said Scooter, still holding the knapsack.

"Did you have it when you came into the store?" asked the boy, not even trying to keep the patronizing tone out of his voice.

"I . . . I think so."

"Maybe you left it in your car," the boy said. "Some people don't like to sit on their wallet and they take it and put it on the seat beside them, or on the dashboard, except then when the car goes around a turn, the wallet slides down to the floor so you had better look there too." He took a breath.

"I'm riding a motorcycle," said Scooter, frantically patting every pocket.

"Well, I'll just take that pack"—the boy reached over and snatched it from Scooter's grasp—"while you go look for your wallet. I'll keep it for you, behind the counter, and when you have some money you can come back and it will be waiting for you."

Scooter Loon found himself unable to let go of the leather strap.

"I want to hold this awhile," he said.

"I think you had better let go, sir," said the college boy, looking quickly around for a security guard.

Because things had always gone Scooter's way, he fancied himself a patient man. In fact, in his dealings with his classmates and friends, in his relationship with his parents, and in his love for Faranak he was that way, forbearing and generous. But the man's behavior, in tandem with his fears about his wallet, his life, and his mother, was just too much, and Scooter Loon lost control. He pulled on the strap as hard as he could, and the boy came toward him, over the glass countertop, his face screwed up in anger. When he was very close, his nose nearly touching the Loon's, Scooter let go suddenly like sneaky schoolchildren sometimes do to each other. The alligator shirt fell back against the display case behind him, still clutching the sack. The force of his weight shattered the glass. All of a sudden there were alarm bells and security personnel appeared, wearing what seemed to the bewildered son of Adam and Sharon Steinberg to be pharmacist jackets.

"Has he stolen anything?" demanded one of the pharmacists.

The alligator boy shook his head but seemed unable to speak.

"You will have to leave the store, sir," he said, taking Scooter firmly by the arm and leading him downstairs and out.

"But my wallet," Scooter said.

"Did you leave it at the counter, sir?"

"No. I can't find it."

"That is unfortunate." With this the man let go of Scooter's arm and marched back inside. Scooter found himself to be the object of considerable curiosity in the parking lot. Never had so many people wanted to look at him and tried so hard not to.

With the wallet still missing, Scooter was forced to take his belongings from the back of the bike and spread them out on the lush green grass in front of the store. It was probably the sight of his underwear that drew the Freeport police cruiser to the scene. The cop stopped his car and emerged, slamming the door behind him and swaggering over to where Scooter stood, pensively surveying his belongings.

"This your stuff?" said the cop.

Scooter had been lost in a mental reconstruction of his day and was startled when the lawman spoke.

"Uh, yes, Officer, it's all mine. I'm trying to find my wallet."

"Bad place to spread your things, particularly personals, if you know what I mean," said the officer, bending to where Scooter's motorcycle jacket lay and then kneading the leather in his hands. "Do you have any identification?"

"Sure I do," Scooter Loon replied, suddenly conscious of his eleven fingers, "but it's all in my wallet, which I can't find."

"This wouldn't be the wallet in question?" said the policeman, tilting his mirrored sunglasses down until they rested on the bridge of his nose and staring at Scooter Loon with an outstretched hand.

Scooter looked down to see his billfold.

"Jacket, vest pocket," the cop explained. "Happens all the time. Put it there and then can't feel it through the material. Good place to keep it though, hard for a pickpocket to reach, particularly when the zipper is closed, not that Freeport is full of bump-and-run types."

"I'll remember that," said Scooter Loon.

"What type are you?" asked the cop, withdrawing Scooter's driver's license and his university identification card.

"I don't like to think of myself as a type," said Bernard Steinberg.

"You go to Yale?" said the cop, raising his eyebrows slightly.

"I did," said Scooter Loon, valedictorian of his business school.

"You drop out?"

"Graduated," said Scooter, staring at the cop as hard as he could, feeling the anger coming again.

"Just taking a little time off, eh? Well, enjoy yourself, ride carefully." He handed the wallet back to Scooter. "And one more thing."

"Yes?"

"Pick up your underwear," said the strong arm of Freeport, Maine.

Scooter spent that second night in the Boothbay area, in a place called Newagen, down near the bottom of one of coastal Maine's larger peninsulas. He found a large ramshackle inn there with a vast lawn and a long saltwater pool cut out and walled off from the beach. The overnight price was too high, so he secreted his Ducati in the woods by the edge of the property and spent the sunset scanning the sea for whales. Tiny black flies beset him as the sunlight fled, and he took refuge in his mummy bag, all zipped up tight, his feet touching the rear tire of his mount. He could feel the hard rubber through the down and the sensation comforted him almost as much as the slight firmness of the wallet crammed against his hip.

He awoke once during the night and was sure that hotel security was going to kick him out, but it was only a raccoon, his yellow eyes very close and bright. Scooter stared back, without saying anything, and in the end the animal went away. As he drifted off again Scooter wondered vaguely whether raccoons could identify and pilfer wallets. He also thought about Faranak, and he felt very sad as he tried to envision her face when he told her that he did not want her for a wife.

Scooter spent his third day out enjoying the shops and streets of Boothbay, and he spent another night amid the pines of Newagen. He was plagued, however, by a nagging feeling that he should not be out of touch so long. By the morning of the fourth day the feeling was terrible and intense, and so Scooter Loon took out his map and plotted the fastest way back to the freeway.

The return drive to New Haven was a grueling exercise in concentration and the tolerance of back pain. The splendid race suspension of the Ducati that had allowed Scooter victory from Baja California to East Rock Road was deadly stuff on the long straight haul, and several times Scooter had to hop off in pain and frustration, screaming into his helmet. When he finally made the Yale campus it was nearly three o'clock in the morning, and everything was covered by a tight mist. Exhausted, he clumped up the stairs to Faranak's room, thinking that it was time to tell her that he was not the perfect Persian she would like him to be, and that he really had to love himself before he could love someone else.

He fidgeted a few moments, trying to make his sore and tingling fingers work the key in the lock. When he opened the door he saw Faranak sitting in her favorite rocking chair, a dim and yellow reading light illuminating her face. The chair was turned to face the door, and Scooter Loon saw that

Faranak's eyes were puffy and her face was stained with tears. At that moment he knew he had to tell her the truth, if only so that he could live with himself.

"I'm sorry," he began.

Faranak just shook and shook and shook her head. "Oh, my silly man," she said. "I am the one who is sorry. I am sorry because I have to tell you that your Mother Loon is dead."

21

The Los Angeles County port of San Pedro, where Biji Steinberg quite literally embarked on her first modeling job, is frequented by huge tankers with fronts that open like gigantic gulping guppies. These ships carry all manner of heavy goods, particularly cars from Japan and Korea, as well as oil, typewriters, drill presses, and bananas. The port is also significant in that it is the send-off point for the products of the infamous baby gang's regular operations. The leader of the baby gang, who had once been married to Clea and who had passed up the chance to steal Scooter Loon on account of his misfingering, liked San Pedro. The number of babies he had exported from the port was probably almost equal to the number of orchids in Harlan Kowalski's collection.

Harlan was the baby-gang leader's right-hand man, his confidant, and his director of operations. It was Harlan who twenty-four years earlier had flatly rejected Bernard Steinberg on the basis that eleven-toed boys don't sell. Far more so than the leader of the baby gang, Kowalski was a criminal mastermind. While the baby-gang leader had the flair and charisma that is required to lead men, it was Harlan who had the mind for detail, the methodical, deadly cunning that is required of the professional kidnapper. The baby-gang leader liked to think of his operation in corporate terms. In his scheme of things Harlan was the chief operations officer while he himself was the chairman of the board.

Because he was so good at his job, the entire gang was surprised when Kowalski botched the transfer and sale of the infant later to be known as the banana bantling.

In all fairness to Harlan, he had not really been the one to bungle the transfer of the stolen child and leave the baby lying screaming on the pier swaddled in a banana crate. To be sure, he was ultimately responsible for choosing to do business with men who represented themselves as legitimate baby buyers and who in the end couldn't come up with a single peso, but Harlan physically performed his end of the delivery without flaw.

When Harlan's crew returned from the drop spot without any money, they rushed back to the pier to reclaim the infant only to find the area swarming with police cars. They reported back to Harlan in terror. The chief operations officer gave a very flat rendition of the screwup to his flamboyant leader.

"It was a no-show," said Harlan, maneuvering an antacid tablet past his monstrous mustache and into the swells and passages of his massive belly.

"Well, we'll sell the kid somewhere else, that's all," said the baby-gang leader, sipping a peach Margarita that had just been unemotionally prepared for him by his new toy robot.

"Can't do that," said Harlan. He slipped his thumbs into his denim overalls like a fat pig farmer.

"Why not?"

"Don't got the kid no more," the operations man replied.

The baby-gang leader looked up at Harlan. "You need to get new clothes, Harlan. I've been telling you that for twenty-five years, but you're getting worse and worse. You look like a pig farmer."

"Cops got the kid," Kowalski told him.

"What!" the baby-gang leader screamed.

"Pickup fell through. Kid cried on the dock. Cops got the kid."

The baby-gang leader began to inhale and exhale fiercely through the plastic straw that he had stuffed into his too-frozen drink.

"Cops got the kid," he repeated over and over. "Cops got the kid."

"Feds got called in," said Harlan.

"How do you know?"

"Police band."

The baby-gang leader seemed to Harlan to be very upset, rocking back and forth and sucking like an idiot, but in fact the man was secretly pleased. Things had died down since the kidnapping of the Japanese consul's child in San Francisco, and the gang leader's self-destructive, bored side was on the wax again.

"Any ties, anybody see anything? Any loose ends to worry about?"

"Only the buyers, Argentines, and they've flown. Probably couldn't come up with the green."

"So no loose ends," said Clea's former husband. He struggled not to let on, but he was a little disappointed that he had nothing to worry about.

The banana-bantling case report automatically came across Special Agent Niles Grosbeak's computer and he began reading it with interest. When he finished the status and summary and dove into the details, he felt the hairs on the back of his neck beginning to prickle and rise. He couldn't quite put his finger on it, but something, call it the intuition of a seasoned lawman, told him that he was looking at the work of the familiar baby gang. He memorized the specific circumstances of the case and then set off for the scene of the crime.

The parent of the banana bantling lived in a suburban housing tract not far from MacArthur airfield in Santa Ana, California. Melissa Midwhittle was a breeder of American Staffordshire bull terriers, and while her house appeared tranquil and undistinguished from the front, her backyard was filled with hardened-steel chain-link fences, the sort that are required to adequately contain the parent stock of the pit bull fighting dog.

Melissa was a twenty-nine-year-old divorcée. Despite her ex-husband's legal protestations, she had managed to gain custody of her infant son by proving that she had a secure and stable home in which to raise him. When gaunt Grosbeak pulled up in his unmarked domestic sedan, Melissa noticed immediately. Since the theft of her baby, returned now after being identified by his fingerprints, she had become paranoically watchful of events on the street.

Niles emerged birdlike from the sedan and strode casually over to the front of Melissa's house, looking from the sprinkler system to the roof and back again, letting his eyes run down the alley along the side of the building. The moment he set foot on the green limits of Melissa's lawn, the killer terriers in the yard set up a fearful yapping. Niles simultaneously marveled at the testicles of the man who had stolen the banana bantling and felt in his heart that he was dealing with the gang that had foiled him everywhere from San Pedro to San Francisco.

Melissa Midwhittle was surprised to see another investigator. She had seen more policemen come through her door in the four days her baby had been missing than most people see in a lifetime of watching movies and television. She had spent hours answering questions about her daily routine and describing her little boy, but amazingly had never been quizzed on what she considered to be the most germane of all puzzles: Why her baby?

"The name's Grosbeak," Niles said, offering his identification to Melissa's peephole. The breeder unbolted the series of locks and deadbolts that she had installed since the theft of her son and opened the door a crack to look at Niles's face.

"What do you want?" she said. "Haven't I answered enough questions?"

"We are still looking for the perpetrator, ma'am," said Special Agent Grosbeak. "I'd like to try to find out more than the other men have so that something terrible like this doesn't happen to some other unsuspecting mother."

"Come in," said Melissa Midwhittle, using her foot to move the Staffordshire that stood, fangs bared, growling behind the door.

Niles sat warily on the sofa while Melissa put some hot water on the stove.

"Brutus won't hurt you," she called. "Just stay where you are and don't move around."

Grosbeak, by nature a pacer, felt distinctly uncomfortable and kept his hand on his revolver as he was stared down by the thrumming dog.

"The main question I have," said Grosbeak, twisting in on the couch a little, which seemed to upset the dog, "is why the kidnapper chose your baby to steal."

"Well, it wasn't my ex-husband who did it," said Melissa, appearing with some tea that looked and smelled like licorice water. "He hasn't got the balls for this kind of thing."

"No, we know he wasn't involved." Grosbeak smiled weakly.

"Not that he wouldn't love to pull off something like this," Melissa added.

"But with these dogs"—Niles smiled—"it just seems that it would be rather difficult to sneak in here and take a sleeping child."

"You know," said Melissa Midwhittle, "you're the smartest man they've got in the FBI."

Niles inclined his head, which was all he dared do with Brutus watching.

"I mean you're the first person to ask me the 'why' question. Everyone else had been very worried about who and how."

"I believe that one leads to the other," said Niles, "and so I'd like to reconstruct every single thing that you did in the ten days before your baby was sna— was abducted."

"I just want to go check on him," said Melissa, disappearing for a moment and leaving Niles in the company of Brutus once more. When she showed up again she was carrying the banana bantling.

"Beautiful baby," said Grosbeak, trying his brittle best to be charming. "He takes after his mother."

Niles spent the entire day with Melissa Midwhittle, reconstructing her every move. He made her tell him where she shopped, who cleaned her drapes, whether she had experienced problems with her telephone or appliances lately, where she went out to eat, who her boyfriends were, what family members came to visit or called, even what medications she took and what pharmacy supplied them. He wanted to know whether she took care of her own dogs or whether she had kennel help, and he wanted to know all about her veterinarian and any people that worked for him that might have come to the house.

Maybe because she was a housebound divorcée who received little attention from men, Melissa Midwhittle found Special Agent Grosbeak highly attractive. She plied him with cookies and strange-smelling teas, and went to the rest room often to brush her hair and gargle with mouthwash. Niles was unaccustomed to a woman's attentions and found himself enjoying the interrogation. What he enjoyed even more, however, was zeroing in on the baby gang.

"So this big fat man with a mustache delivered your dog food for you," said Niles.

"And it was kind of strange," said Melissa Midwhittle. "I always get my own food, you know, and then load it into my hatchback. This was the right brand, but not the exact same food I use."

"Did you call the pet shop to verify that they had sent out the order?" asked Niles.

"No, I . . ."

"My guess," said Niles Grosbeak suddenly, "is that if we call we will find that the delivery man did not come from your pet shop. I would also warrant"—Niles paused dramatically—"that the food contained some sort of sedative."

"Now that you mention it, they have been kind of subdued lately." Then she covered her mouth. "Oh my God," said the mother of the banana bantling.

"I would further warrant," said Niles, standing up with a victorious look on his face, "that your baby was stolen precisely because your dogs made him such a challenging target."

After the police artist had spent two hours with Melissa Midwhittle and the Identikit, Niles Grosbeak sat sipping licorice tea and staring at a remarkably good likeness of Harlan Kowalski. Finishing his snack as quickly as he could, the G-man kissed Ms. Midwhittle gently on the cheek and went downtown to look at the mug books.

To his everlasting misfortune and contributing to his ultimate demise, Kowalski was no stranger to the inside of a jail cell. He had spent two days in the Los Angeles County lockup for urinating on the side of a police cruiser while in a drunken and disorderly state. Even though the photo was many years old, the trained eye of Niles Grosbeak picked him out at once. The mug book listed Harlan as a resident of the scenic but foggy town of Morro Bay on California's central coast.

Harlan had lived in Morro Bay since he was a boy and still occupied the house left to him by his parents in their will. From the outside the place looked as if it might be haunted. There were dormers with tiny round windows and gables and flat black roofing tiles. The sides were painted wine-red, and while the base was small, the house climbed sharply skyward like the outstretched neck of a curious chicken.

The exterior belied Harlan's interior decorating. Most of the rooms were simple, modern, and bare. Harlan slept in one room, used the kitchen for cooking and eating, and spent no time whatsoever in the living room or den. Most significantly, he had converted an upstairs bedroom to a sophisticated computer nerve center for the nefarious activities of the baby gang.

While Harlan's pig-farmer appearance was not the look of the typical computer expert, it certainly was appropriate for work in the greenhouse, which had earned him his moniker. The arboretum stuck off of the side of the house like an erect finger, and it was here, amid the *Phalaenopsis, Cymbidia, Cattleya,* and *Miltonia,* that Harlan spent every leisure moment. In short, when Harlan Kowalski was not plotting the abduction of infants for resale, monitoring the police bands on his radio, or tapping into law-enforcement computer banks, he was spraying, bagging off buds, and repotting his beloved orchids.

When Niles Grosbeak pulled up in front of Harlan's house, the fat man was deeply involved in a hybridization procedure, trying to cross a common *Vanilla* plant with a tight-lipped

African miniature from the forest floor in hopes of producing
both fine bouquet and color. The greenhouse was quiet, however, and despite his attention to the pistils and stamens,
Harlan heard the FBI car instantly. He stripped off the rubber
gloves that he used to protect himself against insecticide and
rushed to the peephole just in time to see Grosbeak, wearing
black rubber-soled police shoes, climb the short front walk.
Without skipping a beat, Harlan made for the garage, where
his souped-and-blown black BMW waited for his command.
He started the car, raised the door, and was squealing out onto
the roadbed before Niles had a chance to ring the doorbell.

When he saw the tire smoke and heard the gears whine,
Grosbeak knew at once that he had the right man. He sprinted
to his car and gave chase, following Kowalski through the
twisting foggy streets of Morro Bay and onto the freeway. The
BMW fairly flew north along the Pacific Coast Highway, and
it was all Niles could do to keep his car on the road and try to
radio for help. The population of FBI agents in the central
coast area is low, so Niles ended up calling out his position and
radioing for assistance from the local highway patrol station.

Grosbeak never guessed that Harlan had turned on his own
police scanner and was eavesdropping on the entire capture
plan. Despite his unkempt appearance, the operations man
was a tireless and thorough strategist, and he had plotted his
escape route many years before, keeping it current by driving
it every month or so. The race-bred sports sedan was far more
at home on the twisty coastal road than Grosbeak's vehicle.
Niles tired quickly as the horizon dipped and twisted, revealing occasional views of the cold gray Pacific through his
window. Several times the policeman felt his fender scrape the
rocks on the right side of the road and struggled in fear as
the rear wheels fishtailed across the dividing lane and into the
path of oncoming traffic.

It was nearly dusk as the speeding pair reached Cambria,
and officers from the San Simeon area joined the chase, forming a line of screaming black-and-whites behind the kidnapper's machine. As the coastline's curves got tighter and
tighter, Harlan gained more and more of a lead, until there

were times, with the twists and turns of the road, when it was a full half minute before he saw any lights in his mirror.

At one point along the coast the crags and irregularities of the shoreline combine with the tides to make the coastal edge impassable. Here, in the vicinity of a beach called Limekiln, the road snakes away from the water and passes onto a high bridge. Not far from the bridge there is a small dirt off-branching, and it was here that Harlan turned, slowing to almost a snail's pace before exiting the roadway in hopes of leaving no tire marks or tracks.

Kowalski had planned his escape route so that the turnoff would not be noticed by police cars directly on his tail. Pursuers would miss his quick turn because it came directly after a sharp corner. True to his predictions, three California Highway Patrol chase cars sped right by the driveway into which he had turned. When they had passed Harlan motored gently to the inconspicuous ingress to a large cave. He covered his car with a pile of loose sagebrush, which he had cut some months before, and went into the cave. The hiding place was equipped with a folding cot sealed in plastic, a week's worth of food, lanterns and reading material, a radio with fresh batteries, a generator, an electric heater, and several changes of clothes.

What the kidnapper and master planner had not realized was that the dirt turnoff was visible from one particular spot nearly three quarters of a mile back. Special Agent Niles Grosbeak was just descending the coastal cliffs for the approach to the Limekiln area when, purely by the same sort of chance that characterized everything to do with Scooter Loon, he saw Harlan Kowalski leave the highway. Smiling, the policeman turned off his radio and watched the officers of the California Highway Patrol continue up the coast in hot pursuit.

When he reached the turnoff Niles nosed his vehicle onto the dirt and then got out on foot. He walked up the drive until he came to Harlan's dusty BMW. Moving as quietly as his creaking joints would permit, he withdrew his gun and penetrated the cave where the kidnapper was unpacking his supplies.

Harlan turned quickly and made a quick dive for a Remington shotgun propped against the musty stone. Niles Grosbeak, in a smooth, measured, and consciously savored move, sent a bullet whizzing by Harlan's ear and moved to kick the shotgun out of reach.

"Your mistake," he said as Harlan's hands shot straight up in the air, "was to leave that kid on the dock in the banana crate."

"You can't take me to jail," Kowalski breathed heavily. "What will happen to my orchids?"

"You should have thought of that before you went to Bel Air," said Niles Grosbeak.

"Bel Air?" said Harlan Kowalski, who knew he'd never been there.

22

In remote Iranian towns most women are wed at puberty. Those upper-class Persian ladies who can afford to be educated abroad may hold out until they are out of their teens, but only if she's singularly unattractive is a Persian woman still single at twenty-three. Despite Faranak's attempts to Americanize herself, after four years at Yale she still walked to the beat of a Muslim drum. She was ready, in short, to move to New York City and become Mrs. Scooter Loon. Of course she did not formally propose to Scooter, but she was sure to make both her timetable and her plans well known.

"I can't even think about this now," said the former racer as he packed his things as quickly as possible for the trip to Santa Barbara.

"I know that I shouldn't be talking with you about such serious things at this time, but . . ."

"Then, please, let's leave it," Scooter said, stuffing everything he could into his suitcase.

"Where are you dialing?" said Faranak as Scooter picked up the telephone.

Scooter covered the mouthpiece with his hand. "I'm calling the truckers that brought my bike out here," he said.

"So you will not take the Ducati to New York. Well, Scooter Loon, quite frankly I am glad. I don't think that the Big Pineapple is the place to be riding around, and you will be wearing a three-piece suit there, that's for sure."

Scooter stared at Faranak for a long moment and then put the phone back in its cradle.

"I'm not going to New York," he said. "It's time for me to go home."

"Then, I will find a job in the City of Angels," said Faranak.

"Listen," said Scooter Loon. "I have loved the time we spent together, and I will never forget you, but you must let me go. I cannot marry you. I don't know that I ever want to get married, but I do know that I can't do it now."

"Are you asking me to wait for you?" asked Faranak, watching Scooter's face closely.

"I am asking you to take me to the airplane and kiss me good-bye."

They rode together in silence nearly all the way to Hartford, the nearest large terminal. The car was crammed with as many of Scooter Loon's belongings as he dared to hope the airline would allow. After they had parked and purchased Scooter's ticket, Faranak followed him to the gate.

"You will call me when you get there?" she asked.

"I will call you," said Scooter Loon, knowing full well that he would not.

The new graduate was worried about seeing his father, mainly because he felt terribly guilty about missing his mother's passing, but also because he was afraid of Roman's grief. Despite the fact that the airport in Santa Barbara has a landing strip large enough for jets, there are no mobile corridors, and planes must park several hundred feet from the gate. Disembarking passengers file down folding stairs to the tarmac and then walk the distance to the terminal entrance.

Roman Loon had been waiting in the airport lounge when Scooter was still high over the Rocky Mountains. He had closed Loon Motors for the week of the funeral and sat chain-smoking in a green plastic chair, his pickup truck in the lot outside. When Scooter appeared at the gate, weighed down with all the belongings he could carry, Roman knew he had come back to California to stay, and all the hateful angry things that he had planned to say in castigation fled his mind.

"You look so thin," Scooter said, dropping his bags to embrace the thief who had stolen him from his crib.

"Your mother missed you," said Roman Loon, holding his son at arm's length to meet his gaze.

"I missed her too," said Scooter Loon, "and I'm going to keep on missing her."

The funeral was a quiet affair held at a music academy in the hills behind Santa Barbara. In attendance were some of Scooter's high school and college classmates, loyal Loon Motors customers, and a select few friends of warmhearted Marian Loon, a woman who had devoted herself almost entirely to her family. While kind words were spoken a baroque quartet played the same Vivaldi and Bach pieces that Marian had loved and listened to all her life. Both Scooter and Roman were dry-eyed during the ceremony, but when they returned to the Riviera dwelling Roman looked about at the dust and dark and collapsed completely.

Roman and Marian Loon had married at nineteen, and despite his self-sufficient, macho image, Roman was quite lost without his spouse. Scooter spent a full month helping his father with the apartment, clearing out his mother's things, and making a bachelor dwelling for his reluctant father. Using Loon Motors earnings, Scooter bought Roman a microwave oven and arranged for a maid to come once a week and clean. It was not until Roman had reopened Loon Motors that he broached the subject that Scooter Loon had been dreading.

"Then, I gather you're going to put all that business know-how to work for the bike shop," Roman said with a smile as he twisted the throttle on an old Moto Guzzi motorcycle that was up on his lift.

"I'd be happy to help with a few pointers," said Scooter, looking about the shop with a heavy and familiar feeling.

"You can just take over the books, ads, and inventory," said Roman, not looking at Scooter, his hands buried within the bowels of the old twin-cylinder machine.

"I'm not going to stay and work here again, Dad," said Scooter.

"You've got bigger fish to fry, eh?" said Roman. "You went to school and now you think you know it all."

"Actually, I think I don't know any of it, which is why I

want to get a job and start seeing the world," said the ace motorcycle racer.

"How long do you figure that'll take," said Roman, "your traveling about, I mean?"

"I'm not talking about traveling," said Scooter. "I'm talking about starting my own life somewhere."

"Your Persian girl called this morning," said Roman.

"Why didn't you tell me?"

"It seems to me that when you talk about starting a life somewhere, somehow I don't see her in it."

Scooter sighed.

"She said she was in New York. Are you going to New York?"

"No," said Bernard Steinberg. "I'm going to Los Angeles."

Business school contacts garnered Scooter Loon a number of interviews in the City of Angels. Scooter went to each on his Ducati, which had arrived unscathed from the East Coast. He dressed in stylish but appropriate garb, but his hair was squashed flat from his motorcycle helmet.

The first two interviews were with the California offices of investment banking firms. These establishments were interested in training Scooter Loon for assignments abroad or on Wall Street, and they did not go well. The interviewers were stiff and slow-witted, and Scooter found himself bored by them. When he reached a certain level of disgust, approximately twenty minutes in, Scooter began to talk about motorcycle racing.

"The most dramatic thing," he began, "was the time I saw goat guts all over the road in Mexico when I was doing a hundred and fifty miles an hour. Can you imagine what wet intestines do to your traction?"

This of course signaled the end of the conversation.

The third interview was with a tire company, interested in Scooter because of his unique combination of business training and racing reputation. They wanted his help in their marketing department, and Scooter was generally interested. The problem was that the tires were of poor quality, and in the end Scooter decided against lending his name, such as it was, to an inferior product.

The fourth interview was with one of the major Japanese motorcycle manufacturers. Scooter had studied the history of this company while at Yale and had gained a great deal of respect for its operations. In addition to motorcycles, the company manufactured missiles, pianos, thermometers, and computers and was noted for its avant garde management policies. In the end, however, Scooter proved to be too much of an individual to work for the team. His arrival at their door on an Italian motorbike sounded a death knell from which he never quite recovered.

Scooter's fifth interview was a resounding and utterly unexpected success. It was with an advertising agency run by a former Yale student and a friend of his business school adviser. Unbeknownst to Scooter, this professor had personally called the agency. He told its president, a man named Gabriel Peterman, that he must not let Scooter Loon slip through his fingers.

"Offer him a palace in the San Bernardino foothills if that's what it takes to get him," said the old man. Peterman was astounded. He had never heard the dour old educator give anybody anything but the most sparing recommendation, and he was fascinated by Bernard Steinberg before the six-fingered racer ever entered his office.

"What we do here," Peterman explained, "is create corporate or project images."

"You mean themes for an ad campaign," said Scooter.

"More than just themes, although we do analyze the marketplace to figure out the best motif. We thread the nuts and bolts as well. We decide on the media to be used, the timing, the sequence, everything."

"If you were in politics," said Scooter Loon, "you'd be kingmakers."

"Precisely," said Gabriel, pleased to see how fast Scooter caught on.

"So the job would have many facets, from market analysis to the details of production."

"As many facets as you can handle."

"And the pay?" asked Scooter.

"I haven't offered you the job yet." Peterman smiled.

"I didn't gather we were talking about some mythical person here," said Scooter. "What about the pay?"

Gabriel Peterman named a figure.

"I'd rather pump gas and ride my motorcycle through the mountains on weekends," said Scooter.

"I don't believe you," said the adman.

Scooter had listened carefully to the lectures in his "contracts" class, and he knew well how much money was generally left on the table in corporate negotiations. "Give me a call when you really need me," he said, standing to leave.

Peterman cleared his throat and doubled his figure.

Scooter sat down again. "Now things are getting interesting," he said.

"You'd better be worth it," Gabe Peterman said.

"You wouldn't have offered it to me if you didn't know I was," said Scooter Loon.

"When can you start?" asked the executive.

"How soon do you need me?"

"Right away. We're starting a new project that I think might interest you."

"I'll need to find a place to live," said Scooter, thinking of the ride back up to Santa Barbara in Los Angeles rush-hour traffic, "and I'll need you to pay for my move down from Santa Barbara."

"No problem," said Peterman.

"I'll also need a cash advance to put a wardrobe together," said Scooter.

"And a car allowance, I'd expect."

"No thanks," said Scooter. "I'll just ride my bike."

"Won't look too good—" began Peterman.

Scooter silenced him with a hand. "The way I get around is on two wheels," he said. "Tell me about the new project."

"We're going to drop you into the Los Angeles business

game like a skinned cat into hot oil." Gabe smiled. "I'm going to put you to work on promoting a movie."

"What's the film about?" asked Scooter.

"It's a police comedy based on the story of the kid they found at the docks in San Pedro, the one they call the banana bantling."

"Isn't kidnapping children a pretty passé topic?" asked Bernie Steinberg.

23

Although he could have afforded more posh surroundings, Scooter chose a small but elegant loft in a modern building in the Santa Monica section of Los Angeles County. There was covered parking for his prized Ducati, and the ocean was just across the street. Sometimes, when the wind blew from the east and picked up the detritus of the valley, the sky turned orange outside of Scooter's ledges and deposited a brown silt on the window seams. On days like these Scooter felt depressed and gazed out over the tops of the palms to the open expanse of the Pacific. He looked for whales and he thought of his mother and sometimes of Faranak.

The Loon commuted to work by heading east on surface streets rather than braving the steaming horror of the L.A. freeway system. His office was on the seventh floor of a shiny new Hollywood office building, and he was protected from assault and injury by a security guard at hall's end and by two lesbian secretaries who made a tight and formidable team.

Amazingly enough, Gabriel Peterman gave Scooter leave to orchestrate the banana-bantling campaign as he saw fit. Drawing upon what proved to be an unerring instinct for knowing what would stop people in their tracks, Scooter immediately concocted a strategy. Kidnapping, he reasoned, was not only a repugnant crime, but one that every parent and every child feared. The catch phrase for the movie promotion thus became "IT COULD HAPPEN TO YOU," coupled with a picture of a wailing infant with tearing eyes struggling to free himself from the confines of a banana crate. Scooter made extensive use of short television commercials that flashed only the familiar bantling photo and an ominous narrative voice repeating the catch phrase. This was followed by a white screen with black letters announcing that the film, starring Reno Raven and Lee Frisk, was coming soon.

Gabe Peterman was a man enraptured. Not only had his gamble on Scooter Loon paid off magnificently, but the impact of the bantling commercials, as well as the attendant billboard, magazine, and newspaper ads, was giving him more Hollywood movie business than he could handle.

"The producer wants to meet you," Peterman told Scooter Loon. "He's asked us both to a pool party Saturday afternoon."

"I have some plans for Saturday," said Scooter. "Somebody is delivering a big plant for me. They don't usually deliver, but this fellow's making a special trip."

"What kind of plant?" asked Peterman.

"I've arranged for a sagebrush for the living room," said Scooter Loon.

"Sage won't grow indoors," said Peterman.

"I'm going to try it with special lighting," Scooter told him. "It's the only plant I have."

"Why not choose something easier?"

"I like the smell," Scooter told him. "It's sort of a good luck thing with me."

"Then you should put it in the bedroom," Gabe Peterman said with a wink. "Just don't miss the party. I don't want to blow the account because of some weed. Besides, you'll get to meet a movie star or two. The party's being held at Reno Raven's pool."

When Reno Raven heard that Murray Feldman was planning to cancel the bantling movie out of injured male pride, he immediately threatened to sue. Promotions were everywhere, he argued, and to drop the project now would damage everyone's reputation, particularly his own. These threats, combined with the persuasive powers of Biji Steinberg and lawyer Adam, who got involved to save the film and aid his daughter, caused Murray to relent and save the production. As a gesture of detente, Reno came up with the pool-party idea, and he invited friends and relatives, as well as Sharon and Adam Steinberg, to his Beverly Hills bash.

When people are disturbed or depressed they either pay compulsive attention to their personal appearance and surroundings or they let them go completely to seed. Having endured the absolute nadir in her relationship with her parents, Biji fell into the former category. The morning of the gala, Biji had been to her favorite Malibu hairdresser for a make-over. The man had permed her thick auburn locks until they framed her face in tight curls. The change suited her, primarily by making her appear less of a girl and more of a woman. The short hair accented her high cheekbones and bow lips and made her beguiling and mismatched eyes stand out more intensely than ever.

Biji began the drive down the coast to Beverly Hills at the same time that Scooter Loon eased his Ducati out of the garage and up the shore for Wilshire Boulevard. Moving south near lunchtime, Biji's green Cadillac was slowed to a crawl by traffic.

The siblings made the turn east side by side, but they did not see each other. Scooter was watching for potholes and looking for an opening in the traffic, and Biji had tilted her rearview mirror down and to the left so she could check her look. The siblings proceeded out of Santa Monica and into West Los Angeles, the sun high overhead.

Wilshire Boulevard cuts a four-lane swath through West L.A., widening and contracting to accommodate the input of freeways and the in-branchings of parallel roads. It was at one of the narrower sections that Biji Steinberg, driving slightly ahead and to the right of Scooter Loon, came upon a furniture delivery truck stopped dead in the right-hand lane. Its loading ramp was down and couches were protruding. Biji checked her rearview mirror, which showed nothing but her curls, and without looking over her shoulder, swung into the lane to her left.

A motorcyclist who chooses to ride his machine on the street is in considerably more danger than one who elects to test his mettle on the track. The racer must use his mental computer to judge distances, banking, the quiver of forks and tires, the pulsing and roaring of his engine, and the options and decisions of other riders. There are numerous variables on the track, but not so many as on the street, and Scooter Loon knew from bitter experience that despite the lower speeds, the road can be the far more perilous place. He did not laugh when physician friends of his referred to his Ducati as his "donorcycle."

When Scooter saw the truck in the right-hand lane, years of street-riding experience told him to drop back, just on the off chance that the emerald-green 1967 Coupe de Ville should swing into him rather than stop and wait patiently for a break in the traffic. As he always did, Scooter checked his mirrors before he slowed. To his chagrin he noticed that a Mercedes-Benz limousine with blacked-out windows and twin antennae was riding a scant five feet behind him. In the three seconds that passed before his sister pulled out and nearly killed him, he noticed that the lane to his left was full of cars heading straight for him.

Biji was worrying about the confrontation between Reno Raven and Murray Feldman. She had thus far managed to avoid being with them when they were together, letting them hammer out contract work and screen issues with her agent and the film's director. It never occurred to her that a man with eleven fingers and eleven toes was riding a flaming-red Ducati motorcycle in her Cadillac's blind spot.

As soon as Biji moved into his lane, Scooter saw that his only chance was to swing left and ride the center line between Biji's car and oncoming traffic. Knowing that the black limo was nearly upon his rear wheel, he accelerated at the same time he swerved, trying to find himself safe space in front of the green Caddy. His timing was nearly perfect, and he would have emerged unscathed had Biji not moved over farther than was really necessary.

The left front fender of Biji's Coupe de Ville crunched the swooping fiberglass bodywork of the Ducati, making a sickening sound and pinning Scooter's right leg against the frame. The force of the blow sent the Ducati skittering sideways, and it was all Scooter Loon could do to grit through the pain and keep the bike upright and on the center line. The powerful Italian engine was intact, as were all working parts of the bike, and the racer guided the machine to the side of the road, stuck his left foot out, and parked. Using his hands to pull the dented fiberglass away from his leg, Scooter rolled up his shredded trousers to reveal an angry but bloodless welt that ran from ankle to knee.

Biji felt her vehicle shudder slightly with the impact, and her heartbeats came in rapid bursts. Perspiration pricked up on her scalp and her hands turned to ice as she swerved away from the motorcycle and followed it to the roadside. The black Mercedes limousine flashed past.

Scooter dismounted, removed his helmet, put down the sidestand shakily, and leaned back against a parked car. He watched, still trembling, as Biji emerged from behind the wheel and rushed over. Scooter noticed her swells and curves, and then he noticed her mismatched eyes. He didn't recognize her from the pictures he had seen because of her new hairstyle.

"My God, I never saw you," said Biji, all in a jumble.

"You took my lane," said Scooter Loon. "I was just driving along and suddenly you took my lane."

"I swear I never saw you," Biji repeated, brushing her hair back as she became suddenly aware that Scooter was very good-looking.

"I believe you," said Scooter, bending to examine his beloved steed and trying not to stare at Biji.

"I'm sure you didn't do it on purpose."

"I swear I never saw you," said Biji for the third time.

Scooter looked at her and felt his breath get suddenly ragged.

"Are you all right?" she asked. "Let me see your leg."

"It doesn't look great," he said, "but nothing's broken." He turned his injured calf to Biji as if he were modeling lingerie.

"Jesus," said Biji, reaching her hand to touch the raised welt.

The feel of her cool hand set Scooter atingle.

"Actually, it doesn't hurt at all," said Scooter. "I think I must be in shock."

"You're in shock?"

"I think so," said Scooter.

"You don't look like you're in shock, the way you're standing and talking."

"I think I'm in shock but I'm distracted," said Scooter Loon.

"You don't look pale," said Biji.

"That's because I have a suntan from lying on my balcony in Santa Monica."

"I do that too," said Biji.

"Lie on your balcony in Santa Monica?"

"In Malibu. My balcony's in Malibu."

"You must be an actress," said Scooter Loon. "Any girl that looks like you and drives a Cadillac that matches one eye must be an actress. Either that or you have a rich daddy."

"Both," said Biji. "And I'm afraid there's a very important casting meeting that I'm late for."

"Well then, I'll just take your license number and your telephone and let you go," said Scooter Loon.

"My telephone? Why do you need my telephone?"

"You can keep the phone, really. It's just the number that I need."

"Very funny," said Biji. "Why do you need my number?"

"To call you and tell you how much it's going to cost to fix my bike," said Scooter Loon.

"But what about my car?" said Biji. "It's going to cost more to fix my car."

"It's a very expensive bike," said Scooter.

"How do I know you didn't run into me? I'm not really sure what happened."

"Uh-oh," said Scooter.

"So maybe it was your fault and you're trying to blame me."

"Do you remember the black Mercedes that passed us?" Scooter asked.

"Yes."

"Well, it so happens that car belongs to my lawyer."

"So?" said Biji.

"He didn't stop because he has to make court," Scooter said. "I waved him on. We both have to testify in a big FBI case."

"Are you a witness?" asked Biji Steinberg.

"I'm the arresting officer," said Scooter Loon. "We're going to testify in the banana-bantling kidnapping case."

"Shit," said Biji. "I would have to run into a cop."

"Look, I don't have time to talk. Just give me your phone number and let me see your license and we'll be done with it."

While Scooter copied out Biji's vital statistics, he tried not to eye her as obviously as she was eyeing him.

"Gotta go to court," said Scooter, hopping back on his bike and switching it to life. "You drive carefully now. Obey the speed limit and watch your mirrors when you change lanes."

Speechless, Biji stood and watched her brother ride away. She had not even noticed anything unusual about his hands.

Reno Raven's swimming pool was 150 feet long, but only one lane wide. Reno took his swimming as seriously as all his physical activities, and his pool was designed for the two hundred laps he did daily. His offer to host the cast party was most significant because Reno Raven was generally too private to entertain.

"You're late," said Murray Feldman, snatching a delicately baked mushroom quichelette as it passed by in the hands of one of the fifteen serving people Raven had hired. "But fortunately so is one of their people."

"I'm sorry," said Biji. "I had an accident on the way over."

"An accident?" said Reno Raven.

"I hit a guy on a motorcycle. A cop."

"You hit a motorcycle cop and you made it to lunch?" said Gabe Peterman. "Truly, Ms. Frisk, your charm knows no bounds."

"He wasn't a motorcycle cop . . . or maybe he was. Anyway, he wasn't on duty," said Biji.

"Did you hurt him?" asked Sharon Steinberg.

"Skinned his leg and dented his bike. A flashy red Italian thing. Pesquiti, I think it was called." She sat down.

"Probably going to cost you," said Adam.

"Pesquiti," said Gabe Peterman.

At that moment Scooter Loon walked up to the table limping slightly. He wore a natty seersucker suit and an open shirt. One leg of his trousers was tattered and his right shoe was demolished.

"My God, here he is," said Murray Feldman.

"I knew he would follow you," said Reno Raven, rising to all of his very intimidating six and a half feet. "What can I do for you, man?" he asked Scooter.

Biji watched transfixed as Scooter offered his hand.

"A pleasure to meet you, Mr. Raven," he said.

"This is my associate, Mr. Loon," said Gabe Peterman, trying his best to maintain his equilibrium.

"You know this guy?" asked Murray.

"He works for me," said Peterman. "This is the man responsible for the banana-bantling campaign."

Biji Steinberg got up steadily and walked around the table until she stood two feet from Scooter Loon. Their gazes locked for a moment, and then Biji slapped her brother across the face so hard that the sound echoed off the surface of Reno's pool.

"I don't think you're funny," she said.

Adam Steinberg, always cognizant of legal ramifications, came up and took his misfingered son by the arm.

"Maybe you can find some sandals for Mr. Loon while I get him a drink," Adam said, giving the black actor a significant look.

"Take off your shoes, man. Take off your coat too. Relax. This is a pool party," Reno cried.

With a smile, Scooter removed his sport coat, shoes, and socks just as his biological father returned with a Bloody Mary in his hand.

"I hope you like it spicy," said Adam, offering Scooter Loon the drink and staring at his extra finger.

"Thanks," said Scooter, wiggling his toes.

Something about Scooter's motion drew Adam's eye to his feet, and it was a true testimonial to his social grace that Adam did not gawk and swoon at the sight of Scooter's digits.

"Hope you enjoy it," he croaked, turning to grab Sharon and pull her aside.

"Look at that man's toes," Adam hissed at Sharon.

The auburn-haired mother of Biji and Bernard peeked around her husband's waist.

"Oh my God," she said.

"Now look at his fingers," Adam hissed again.

"I'm going to faint," Sharon said.

"Don't faint. We have to play this cool."

"I hope you choke on the ice," said Biji, staring daggers at Scooter Loon.

Scooter walked up to Biji and took her hands in his. "I'm sorry I lied to you," he said. "I really was just trying to get your phone number."

Biji relaxed slightly. "It was pretty clever," she said.

"Just as long as you don't use that number," Reno interrupted, clapping Scooter on the back so hard, he almost pitched into the pool.

"I bet he does," said Biji.

"Well, that's nice, to see you two make up," said Adam Steinberg. "Where are you from, Mr. Loon?"

"I grew up in Santa Barbara," said Scooter. "My father has a business there."

"What sort of business?" asked Adam, holding his glassy-eyed and quivering wife up with his shoulder.

"He runs a motorcycle shop," said Scooter.

"You were born there, I gather? In Santa Barbara, I mean."

"I can't remember that far back," said Scooter Loon with a laugh.

24

Although the damage to Scooter Loon's treasured Ducati was minor, the advertising whiz took it as a sign that it was time to retire the machine. Scooter had owned the bike for many years, and despite the skilled ministerings of Roman Loon, its engine was getting tired. The tucked riding position, moreover, took its toll on Scooter, particularly after a long day at the office. Commuting to work on it, he found it caused him musculoskeletal distress. Both his secretaries took eager turns rubbing his pounded elbows and shoulders, but the discomfort endured. Certain romantic fantasies catalyzed his decision to part with the bike.

"Going to take me up on the car allowance then, eh, Scoot?" said Gabriel Peterman.

"Yep," said Scooter.

"What're you after. Mercedes?"

"Nope," said Scooter.

"Ferrari?"

"Nope," Scooter said again.

"What is all this 'yep' and 'nope'? Have you been out picking corn?" Gabe Peterman asked.

"Ever since last week I don't feel quite myself," said Scooter.

"And he doesn't act it," Scooter Loon's secretaries said in unison.

"Ever since Reno's party?" Scooter's boss winked.

"About then," said Scooter.

"Must be love," said Peterman.

"Oooh," the secretaries chorused.

"Don't be ridiculous," said Scooter Loon.

"So what'll it be?" asked Peterman.

"A BMW."

"How plebeian."

"Not to a Santa Barbara boy," said Scooter.

Later that day, with company check in hand, Scooter took his Ducati down to the local BMW motorcycle dealer. Most people don't even know that the famous German manufacturer produces motorbikes, but of course Scooter knew, and he also knew that they had a reputation for staid but solid excellence.

"Beautiful Ducati," said the salesman as Scooter pulled in. "Too bad about the fairing."

"I want to trade it," said Scooter.

"Sure I can't just sell you a bike?" the man said. "Most people like to hold on to a machine like that."

The motor-sport community is a surprisingly small one, with the same limited number of faces appearing time after time. Devotees of the sport are passionate, however, and their enthusiasm runs deep. Although Scooter's racing career had lasted only a few years, his style and skill, and his triumph over faster and more sophisticated Japanese multicylinder machines using only his little Ducati for a weapon, had earned him a legendary reputation.

"I've had my fun on it," said Scooter.

"A very familiar-looking bike," said the salesman.

"I've ridden it here and there," said Scooter.

"Ever raced it?" asked the man, staring at Scooter curiously.

"It's been well taken care of," said Scooter. "My father is a Ducati mechanic. You're welcome to check it out."

"Has it ever been on the track?" the man persisted.

"It's a street bike," answered Scooter. "Look for yourself. License plates, turn signals, mufflers, the works."

"I think you've raced it," said the salesman.

"Now why would you say that?" asked Bernard Steinberg.

"Because I think I know you. You're Scooter Loon."

Scooter gave a grin. "You got me," he said. "The bike's been raced, but it's still worth plenty. It's got lots of performance parts, it's in beautiful shape—"

"Of course it's worth plenty!" the salesman cried. "Shit, this thing's famous."

"I don't want a lot of fuss," said Scooter. "One of the new BMW four-cylinders, one with lots of room for two people—"

"The famous racer Loon wants a touring bike?"

"Times change," said Scooter.

"She must really be something. The lady, I mean."

Scooter managed a smile. "She certainly is."

Although Scooter had asked Biji only for her telephone number, he had taken her address from her driver's license and committed it instantly to memory at the site of the accident. After her poolside remark about being sure that he would call, he decided to drive by instead. Scooter sensed immediately that, like himself, his sister was easily bored, and to pique her interest he must be unpredictable. True to the modus operandi he had employed when getting to know Faranak, Scooter Loon began to drive by Biji's Malibu flat at odd intervals and different times of day, hoping for a peep into her personal life.

Unlike his obsession with the girl from Iran, which ultimately turned carnal because of the smell of her, Scooter's interest in his sister was purely quixotic. He didn't really know Biji, although he could still feel the sting of her hand on his face, yet he could not escape her. He stared at her name and her face daily in the new material he was putting together for the banana-bantling campaign. He saw her on television and he saw her in magazines. When he drove to work he saw her on billboards near a wailing boxed baby, and when he switched on the radio he heard her name in ads he himself had penned. He thought her arrogant and fiery, and even though he had lied shamelessly in order to get her phone number, he felt a certain kinship to her.

Biji's apartment building lay at the end of a long, dead-end road that ran along the beach. Although there was no security gate, the number of buildings on the road was small and Scooter's appearance, especially aboard an ocean-blue BMW motorbike, was hard to disguise. Twice in his clandestine monitoring of Biji's dwelling Scooter saw Murray Feldman drive his two-seater Mercedes-Benz along the stretch that led to Biji's. He never saw Reno Raven show up there, however, and he suspected that when Biji and Reno got together they did it at the actor's Beverly Hill's palace.

If Scooter was obsessed with the romance and image of his actress sister, Biji was obsessed with the mystery of Scooter Loon. Every time she tried to find out anything about him, she came up empty-handed. She tried to gain information by calling his company, but she was always patched through to his watchdog secretaries, who would sooner have their teeth yanked than say a word about the Loon. He was, they agreed, the best boss they had ever had, and they weren't about to spread idle talk.

Finally, in desperation, Biji called one of the reporters whom she had spared a beating the night that Reno Raven went berserk. She knew that Scooter Loon was not *Star Life* material, but she figured that gossip hounds had plenty of information sources. She was right.

"He's a motorcycle racer," the reporter told Biji over the telephone. "And a very good one, at that."

"Does he still race?" asked Biji. "I thought he worked for an advertising agency."

"Well, I have articles here that describe him winning zillions of road races, including a real famous one in Mexico. This is some years ago, though. He's pretty good-looking, too, from the pictures. Watch I don't tell Reno!"

"I know you wouldn't," said Biji. "Besides, it's not for me. One of my girlfriends is curious."

"I didn't know you had any girlfriends. Maybe there's another *Star Life* article here!"

"Gotta go," said Biji.

In the weeks following their chance meeting Biji thought too often of Scooter Loon. One night, lying half asleep in Reno Raven's arms, she even murmured his name.

"What!" said Raven, who had been cuddling the beautiful

actress while staring at a suspicious lump on the abdomen of his favorite Doberman pinscher.

"I said I should take up the flute and play to the moon," said Biji, instantly awake.

"You must be eating too many soybeans," said Reno Raven. "Now just relax. You need your beauty sleep."

In addition to the attentions and suspicions of the giant Raven, Biji had to contend with the suffering ego of her neurotic little producer. Although Murray had taken Biji's defection very well for a month or so after the shocking news of her sterility, he was unable to cope with seeing her with Reno on a daily basis. Since the day he tied Biji to the coffee table, Murray had been unable to fulfill the promise of his manhood, and at last his veneer peeled away.

"I think," said Murray Feldman, appearing one morning on the set of the banana-bantling film, "that if you spend another night in that spear chucker's bed, I'm going to lose a big piece of my heart muscle."

"Come on, Murray," Biji answered. "Don't tell me you're still pining for me. Why don't you find yourself some bimbo to put up in the San Fernando Valley and have a good time."

"You're so cruel," said Feldman. "I made you, you ungrateful bitch, and even if you can't have children, you have no business rutting with that guy."

"You did not 'make' me," Biji yelled at him. "That happened when my dad harpooned my mom! All you did was take me for a ride and get me some toothpaste gigs."

"That's it," said Feldman. "I want you out of my apartment by Saturday."

"There you go again," said Biji. "That place is mine, and it's in my name."

"It's mine," yelled Feldman. "I pay the rent, I call the tune."

"Go blow, Murray," said Biji in disgust, storming off the set.

The Saturday in question was only two days away, and de-

spite her bravado, Biji was a little worried that Murray might
be serious. She spent Friday night with Reno, and in the morning she aimed the green Caddy for Malibu Beach.

By this time Scooter had a pretty fair idea of his sister's
routine and knew that Biji usually spent Saturday around the
house. At about the same time that she left Reno's, Bernard
Steinberg headed for Malibu himself.

Biji arrived at her apartment about five minutes before her
brother did. Walking from her covered parking space to her
door, she found articles of clothing strewn on the carefully
manicured grass. The density of the blouses, underwear, jeans,
and cosmetic bottles increased the nearer Biji Steinberg got to
her balcony. Murray's revenge was so childish that at first Biji
did not even realize that the things she saw were hers.

All of a sudden Murray Feldman appeared on the lanai.
"Don't even think you can get in here, bitch," he yelled. "Just
gather your things and go, you mindless whore."

"Mindless whore?" Biji repeated.

"Slut, waif, tramp, get out of here."

"I'm coming up, Murray," said Biji, heading for the stairs.

At that moment Scooter Loon pulled into the drive and
parked his BMW behind a hedge.

"You can't get in," said Murray Feldman. "I've changed the
locks."

At this Biji Steinberg paused and turned around to survey
the lawn. Her Art Deco mirror was there, in fragments, as was
all that was left of her beautiful colored-glass bud vase, complete with a single crushed rose. Beautiful lingerie that Reno
had bought her was strewn with a vengeance about the property, each pieced ripped to shreds by furious fingers.

Biji Steinberg began to cry. "Jesus, Murray," she wailed.

Seeing her in such distress, with her mascara running from
her odd-colored eyes, Scooter Loon stepped from the bushes.
He walked up to where Biji knelt, tight and sobbing, and put
his arms around her gently. She looked up at him and blinked.

"Hey," screamed Scooter Loon at the top of his lungs.
"Aren't you Murray Feldman the famous film producer?"

"Shut up!" Murray Feldman hissed from the balcony.

"Aren't you known for your romances, and aren't you producing that movie that's being advertised everywhere about the kidnapped kid?"

"Shut up!" Feldman yelled again.

"Isn't that the film staring Reno Raven?"

"My God, shut up," screamed Feldman.

"Would you like to go for a ride?" asked Scooter, turning Biji's tear-streaked face to his and gently wiping away her smudges.

"A ride? On your Pesquiti?"

"I don't have the Ducati anymore." Scooter smiled. "I've bought something else, just for you."

"Just for me?"

"I think you'll like it. You can wear my helmet."

With this Scooter led his sister over to his deep blue machine.

"I hear you're very good on a bike," said Biji. "But I have to pick up my stuff first."

"Okay," said Scooter. "If I help you, will you take a ride with me?"

"Is this blackmail?" asked Biji Steinberg, beginning to recover herself.

"I suppose it is," said Scooter Loon.

25

Every day for the first month with Biji, Scooter felt as if he were opening a new door to a different magnificent land. Scooter was accustomed to distancing himself from people. He didn't feel that he had much in common with those around him, and in a pattern set up from his early years with Roman Loon, he kept his thoughts to himself. Scooter always knew what people were going to say before they said it, he read people with uncanny accuracy, and he was rarely either pleasantly or unpleasantly surprised. Over the years he developed a sort of resigned boredom, a disappointed acceptance of the way things were to be for him socially, and this made him somewhat cynical.

Time spent with Biji changed all that. Although her own ray-gun brain was focused in a galaxy different from his own, Scooter knew instantly that he had found someone he could call an equal. Biji knew things just as quickly as he did, and would often predict his own reaction with startling precision. Nobody had ever been able to outguess Scooter Loon, and the experience made him want to weep with gladness.

He found her silly, he found her preoccupied with things that should not have mattered, and he found her insecure about imagined weaknesses, but he did not care. Biji never bored him. She read his moods like leaves of tea, and he loved her.

While Scooter was almost childlike in his eagerness to cherish, Biji was cagier. She felt the energy between them just as clearly as he did, but she found it threatening as well as wonderful. She knew that they thought and felt as two gears in a giant clock, but she found it hard to trust him because she had never trusted anybody.

Partly because she was confused by her feelings, and partly because she knew what was important for her career, Biji remained with Reno Raven and kept her meetings with Scooter a secret. This sorely offended Scooter's moral principles. The misfingered Loon respected Raven as an actor and as a man and felt miserable about sneaking around behind the big actor's back. So persuasive was his sister, however, that he agreed to play along until the bantling film was over. Although he hungered for her madly, Scooter sensed her ambivalence, and being moral and patient, he withheld his touch. Such was the will and character of Scooter Loon.

"Let's eat at Gladstone's," Biji yelled into Scooter's helmet as he pulled up beside her parked car. She had driven several blocks from Reno Raven's retreat for the rendezvous. It was a Sunday morning, and Scooter was looking forward to spending the day with Biji, perhaps even to taking a ride in the mountains.

The former racer pulled the bike gently over to the curb and turned to look at his sister.

"Are you sure?" he said.

A popular fish restaurant with an outdoor patio, Gladstone's was the gathering place of Malibu locals, tourists, and entertainment professionals alike. Biji loved an oyster and egg dish that the restaurant had concocted, and she had been going there with her parents for years. Since the article in *Star Life*, and even more since the inception of Scooter's advertising campaign, Biji had shunned such places when in the company of her new beau. The last thing she needed during the final phases of the bantling production was to be seen with Scooter and somehow have word get back to Reno.

"It's no problem," she said. "I haven't been there in ages, and we're arriving on a motorcycle. Nobody will even look at us twice."

"People always look at you twice," said Scooter Loon.

"You're sweet," said Biji, "but I really think it's okay. None of my friends go there anymore, and I know that Reno's not real big on fish."

"Reno's big on everything," said Scooter.

When they arrived at the valet parking area, Scooter parked
the machine away from the door in a distant corner and gave
an attendant five dollars to keep an eye on it. The couple chose
a large corner booth in the back room against the window that
overlooked the water. Biji ordered her usual seafood scramble
and Scooter had a hamburger.

"I want to take you to the Rock Store today," said Scooter.

"I'm not big on rocks, unless they sparkle." Biji grinned.

"It's not really a rock store," said Scooter, "or it is but
that's not why I go. It's way up in the mountains, and all the
racers go there and people drive like maniacs and sometimes
get killed, but you see the most incredible machinery up
there."

"I don't know," said Biji. "I'm not sure that I want to go so
fast with you."

"I don't think I've been going fast at all," said Scooter.

"I'm talking about on your bike." A smile played on Biji's
lips. "Anyway, I think I have a better idea. I want to go up to
Santa Barbara."

"Ah," said Scooter.

"I want to meet your father," she said.

"He's a very busy man," said Scooter.

"On a Sunday?"

Scooter blew through his lips.

"Look at that girl," said Biji, nodding with her nose at a
curvaceous blonde in a halter top and tiny shorts.

"What about her?" said Scooter.

"Do you think she's good-looking?"

"Yes."

"Do you think she has a good figure?"

"She certainly does," said Scooter.

"Do you think she's beautiful?"

"I would say so, yes," said Scooter.

"Go to Santa Barbara by yourself," said Biji, getting up
from the table.

"Oh, sit down," said Scooter. "You're acting like a spoiled
brat. Anyway, I have no intention of going to Santa Barbara."

"Do you think she's better-looking than I am?" asked Biji.

"Biji Steinberg," said Scooter, taking her hands in his as he often did. "What do you think about my extra finger?"

"I think it's fine," said Biji, "a little small, but fine."

"What do you mean 'a little small'?" asked Scooter.

"Well, you know, it's smaller than the rest."

"That's my pinkie," her brother told her. "This one here is the extra finger."

"If it's not the one on the end, how do you know which is the extra finger?"

"I know these things," Scooter said, waving his hand airily.

"So," said Biji. "Do you think that girl is better-looking than I am?"

"I want you to know something," he said.

"What?"

"I have been a few different places," said Scooter, "and I have always looked at beautiful women."

"I'm sure," said Biji.

"And never, not ever in my entire life, have I seen a woman as elegant, as graceful, as entrancing, and as gorgeous as you."

"You're just saying that," said Biji. "If you really love me, take me to Santa Barbara."

"I promise that I will," said Scooter, "but not this weekend."

Biji frowned.

"I just want to be alone with you," he said. "I don't want to share you with my dad today."

The ride from Malibu to the rock store is famous among California bikers and consists of a series of rises, dips, switchbacks, and grades cut from dry, hot, canyon country. The store itself is of little interest, but the location draws large numbers of people from all over Southern California who have in common a willingness to risk life and limb for the thrill of a tilting horizon.

Biji found the ride to the rock store terrifying. It wasn't so much the sheer velocity that scared her as the proximity of her flesh to the pavement. As long as Scooter kept the motorcycle upright, she didn't mind if he reached 120 miles per hour. What concerned her was the way he rushed into corners, waiting until the last minute to toss the motorcycle over in a sharp lean. Biji sucked in her breath at these moments and used her body-builder arms to squeeze her brother nearly tight enough to crack his ribs.

It was on a particularly tight set of curves, where the big BMW was reduced to a crawl, that Biji felt Scooter suddenly get tense. A moment later he pulled the bike off onto the light brown dirt, ripped his helmet off his head, and cut the ignition.

"What is it?" asked the actress, her voice loud in the sudden stillness.

"Just listen," Scooter said.

Above the buzz of crickets and the gurglings of the water-cooled engine, Biji could just make out a distant howl.

"You stopped for that noise?" she said. "How could you hear it?"

"It's a sound I know in my bones," said Scooter Loon. "It's the howl of three cylinders."

"A special kind of bike?" asked Biji.

"Oh, very special," said Scooter. "A Laverda triple. Perhaps an orange one."

"Mexican?"

"It's made in Italy. Put your helmet on quickly, we have to be ready when it comes by."

Scooter and Biji sat idling for a few moments on the BMW, sweating beneath the Pacific sun and waiting. The sound of the engine in question grew slowly but steadily louder until all at once it was upon them and beyond in a raucous orange flash.

Scooter Loon smoked his tires getting back onto the tarmac, spitting gravel and sand in a line behind him, and began to charge through the twisting canyon in pursuit of the Italian bike. His touring mount was no race machine, however, and particularly with Biji on the back, he felt hard-pressed to keep up.

"This guy's very good," Biji screamed into the wind.

"He's the best," said Scooter, too softly for her to hear.

Although the angles and the pace were electrifying, Biji began to appreciate the rhythm of the ride and saw that the two motorcycles were in a duet, one leading, the other following, the music sheer internal combustion.

"This must be what it feels like to race!" Biji shouted again, beginning to genuinely enjoy herself.

The approach to the rock store straightens into a wide sweeper, and the two motorcycles burst onto that final road side by side. Scooter was just gaining on Roman Loon when the older man put on the brakes and pulled into the parking area.

Scooter stopped behind him and Biji hopped off. He watched his father's back as Roman dismounted and put his trusty Laverda on its stand.

"That thing moves pretty good for an old bike," Scooter said loudly.

Hearing his voice, Roman whirled and smiled broadly. There were lines around his eyes that seemed new to Scooter, and the bright canyon sun seemed to put the baby thief in a new light.

Biji watched in astonishment as the older Loon embraced the younger.

"You wanted to meet my father," said Scooter. "I guess you're going to have your chance."

"Where's your Ducati?" Roman demanded, pushing Scooter to arm's length, his hands on his son's shoulders.

"I sold it, Dad," said Scooter.

"Without asking me first?"

"I needed a bike for two," said Scooter.

Biji was wearing designer jeans and a button-down blouse of apricot silk. The top was unbuttoned just enough to show off the swell of her breasts and her perfect tan skin. Biji shook her auburn curls so that they would fluff and ran her fingers quickly through her hair.

"I think I see why," said Roman Loon.

"We almost came up to see you in Santa Barbara today, Mr. Loon," said Biji. "But Scooter said he didn't want to share me with you."

Scooter began to protest but Roman Loon just dismissed him with a wave.

"He was just leading you on, girl," said Roman, drawing closer. "He knows that I come down here all the time."

"That sounds like something he would do," Biji said.

"I see that you know him well."

"Dad, I'd like you to meet Lee Frisk," said Scooter.

"I'm going to do more than meet her," said Roman, drawing off his riding jacket. "I'm going to kiss her." With this Roman drew Biji close and gently put his lips to her cheek.

"Now I see where Scooter gets his charm," said Biji. "Will you tell me where he gets his name?"

Roman gave a melancholy smile. "It was his mother's idea," he said. "All good things came from his mother. And where are you from, Biji with the odd and beautiful eyes?"

"I grew up in Bel Air," she replied. "That's near Beverly Hills."

"I've been there," said Roman. "Once, long ago."

The threesome had sandwiches, sodas, and coffee. Despite the warm greeting he gave her, Roman Loon had not seen any of Scooter's promotions so he did not recognize the actress until Scooter mentioned the bantling film.

"Who's in it with you?" asked Roman.

"Reno Raven," said Biji.

"The black man?"

"He's really the star, I just play his girlfriend. It's a comedy and he's the detective."

"Doesn't sound like a comedy to me," said Roman. "Kidnapping is no joke."

"Well, the screenwriter had to make up most of the story," said Biji, "because they had no leads for quite a while after they found the baby. Now they do, though. I read this morning that the FBI has caught one of the real-life kidnappers. It says in the paper that the man was part of a gang that operated all over California, stealing babies and then selling them for profit."

"I've got a long ride home, Scooter," Roman said suddenly. "Do you want to ride with me for a ways?"

"We'll head back to the beach with you if you're going that way," said Scooter, startled by his father's abrupt change of mood, "but I don't think we want to go north."

Roman set an unusually sedate pace, as if his mind were elsewhere, which of course it was, and Scooter fell in behind him, guiding the heavy German bike through the turns with unaccustomed restraint. At the coast Roman waved without pulling over and headed home, and Biji and Scooter made for the spot where Biji's Caddy was parked, deep in the heart of Beverly Hills.

As they approached her car Biji removed her helmet and compulsively attended to her hair. Scooter parked the motorcycle and got off to kiss her good-bye. Suddenly the big green door swung open and Reno Raven moved smoothly out of the Coupe de Ville.

"Shit," said Scooter Loon.

"I think I know what's going on here," said Reno. "Won't somebody tell me I'm wrong?" He advanced menacingly on Scooter, who stood his ground, his feet light, his helmet in his hand.

Despite his athletic prowess, Scooter knew he was no match for an angry Reno Raven. Raven was eight inches taller and at least seventy-five pounds of hard, solid muscle heavier. The smaller man was further weakened by the feeling that he and Biji had deceived Raven and that the big stand-up comic deserved better.

"One of my stuntmen told me he saw Lee ride up to Gladstone's on a motorcycle," said Raven. "So I said to myself, how can she be riding a motorcycle when I saw her leave this morning in her Caddy? And I ask this dude to explain that and he says he doesn't know nothing about any Caddy, but he sure knows she wasn't driving the bike, since she was on the back."

"I'm in love with her," said Scooter Loon, slumping into the most tired and unthreatening pose he could muster.

"I'm in love with her too," said Raven. "And she lives with me, and she works with me."

"Reno," said Biji.

"If you beat me up," said Scooter, "she might hate you."

"She might hate me if I don't," said Reno Raven, clenching his fists and moving closer to where Scooter stood ready to swing his helmet into the bigger man's head.

"Stop it, goddamnit," said Biji, rushing to interpose herself between the rivals. "Reno, why am I always stopping you from hurting people? We're not in a movie here. When are you going to get some class?"

The fight went out of the big man's eyes. "They say class is something you're born with," he said, strangely sad. "Maybe I just missed my share."

Scooter Loon stuck out his lower lip and looked at Biji. "You know I'll be waiting," he said.

Reno and Biji got into the car and drove away, leaving Scooter standing by the curb, his helmet dangling from his extra finger.

26

In the wake of Reno Raven's party, Adam and Sharon Steinberg were in a state of shock that persisted for days. It was not the unsettling, blow-to-the-stomach type of shock that people get when they receive unexpected news, but rather the sort of shock that comes from the wholesale and ceremonial dumping of long-forgotten garbage on one's lawn. Sharon had many years ago made her peace with the loss of the infant Bernard, and while she had endured her share of emptiness, she had come through it with only a small scar. She had never really known her son, and she was convinced, after the initial exposure to the handsome stranger, that he could not possibly be Scooter Loon.

Adam, however, was just as strongly convinced that the barefoot young man who had arrived on a motorcycle and toyed with his willful daughter as if she were Play-Doh most certainly had Steinberg blood. Adam found Scooter to be smooth, removed, and possessed of a certain distance and restraint that might have been interpreted as cynicism but which Adam recognized as brains. After arguing the point for several days with his wife, Adam called the long-distance operator and found the number for Loon Motors in Santa Barbara. He had his secretary call to find out the shop hours and to determine whether Mr. Loon himself would be in attendance.

On the Thursday morning following the gala, Adam Steinberg canceled his appointments, fired up his twelve-cylinder Jaguar convertible, and headed up the coast for Santa Barbara. He found Loon Motors, after about fifteen minutes of cruising, nestled in a back street amid a row of lower-income houses. The meticulously painted shop was small, with a large gold sign above the door and the insignias of motorcycle brands, many foreign and defunct, stenciled in the clear plate glass. As he walked into the shop he was greeted by the whine of a drill press and the strong smell of grease.

Because Roman Loon worked on unusual and exotic motorcycles, he had a large stock of parts from England, Italy, Spain, and Germany. Many of these parts were used but serviceable, others were new and wrapped in greasy wax paper, untouched since their day of manufacture some fifty years before. Roman's interest in unique and vintage motorcycles had spread in the years since he had gone into business, and Loon Motors, while remaining a small concern, had gained international repute.

Roman's feeling was that if the machine had run at one time, he could make it run again, and his results were true to his philosophy. Wires, bearings, and pieces were not always available for the bikes that came through his door, so to be sure that he could do the job, Roman had put together a fully equipped machine shop. The former cat burglar, a genius with his hands, was proud to be able to remanufacture items for two-wheelers that had not been ground and formed for aeons. In short, if Roman didn't have it, he could make it.

Adam Steinberg didn't understand any of this, but he did notice that the place was immaculate.

"What can I do you for?" said Roman Loon, appearing as if by magic from behind the clean dark counter, a shop rag in his hands.

"I'm looking for Mr. Roman Loon," said Adam.

"You got him," said Roman Loon, taking in Adam's Beverly Hills clothing, his polished English shoes, and, through the window, the Jaguar parked by the curb.

"Do you work on Jaguars?" asked Adam Steinberg, who, though he had imagined a great and dramatic struggle with the man who had stolen his son, had no clue as to how to make small talk with him.

"This is a motorcycle shop, sir," said Roman, turning and walking back behind the counter. "I'm afraid I can't help you with a busted English car."

"Quite a well-equipped place you have here," said Adam. "Seems you should be able to do something."

"May I ask your name?" said Roman.

"The name is Steinberg," Adam replied, watching for a reaction but getting none.

"Well, Mr. Steinberg," said Roman. "As I've said, this is a motorcycle shop. We don't do car repairs here. The most I can do is offer you a telephone book and see if I can't steer you in the right direction."

"You said we," said Adam, looking around. "I don't see anyone else here."

"I have another mechanic, but he's off today," said Roman Loon, watching lawyer Adam with hard eyes.

"The name Steinberg doesn't mean anything to you?" asked Adam.

"I'm afraid not," said Roman. "Now if you'll excuse me, here's the phone book"—he placed a yellow pages on the counter—"I've got work to do."

"Does the name Bernard Steinberg mean anything to you?" asked Adam.

Roman Loon walked back to the racks of old motorcycle parts and, without looking at Adam, shook his head.

"How about the name Scooter Loon?" said Adam.

Roman moved past Adam to the front door of the shop, picked up the "Closed" sign, and put it in the window.

"I'll bet you've been dreading this day all your life," said the Bel Air lawyer.

"I don't know what you're talking about," said Roman Loon, jewel thief and kidnapper of small children.

"Did you ever think about having his fingers and toes cut," asked Adam, "just so that nobody could identify him later?"

"I've never seen a suit like that on a policeman," said Roman Loon. "The pay must be getting better."

"What's getting better," said Adam, "is the pay*back*." With this he picked up a heavy wrench that was lying on the counter in front of him, turned, and threw it at Roman Loon's head.

"You're no copper, that's for sure," Roman yelled back, ducking the flying tool. "Get out of my shop!"

"I think you are filth," said Adam, leaping to pursue Roman in a run around a grinding machine. "I think you are scum."

"Get the hell out of my shop," threatened Roman, picking up an electric drill and squeezing the button to make the bit spin with a shrill whine.

"How did you hide him?" said Adam. "So close to my home? How did you hide a child with too many fingers and too many toes?"

"Get out of my shop," Roman yelled again, waving the whining drill at the door.

Adam moved back to where a row of bikes stood in a neat line. Putting his hip against a very rare 1959 Ariel Square Four, he bumped it over. The Ariel hit a 1926 in-line Four Cleveland, which in turn toppled into a 1950 Vincent Comet. The bikes went over like dominoes.

"My God," screamed Roman Loon. "Those are priceless machines!"

"Not as priceless as a small, six-fingered boy," Adam yelled back.

Either as a measure of his passion, or as a result of how much he trusted his intuition, Adam Steinberg's ears were deaf to Roman's denials. He may have been a poor father and only a middling squash player, but Adam Steinberg was one sharp attorney. He knew Roman Loon was lying. While Roman rushed over with his hand drill buzzing, Adam began systematically to hack at the vintage motorcycles with a foot-long tire iron.

"Stop!" screamed Roman, trying to get at Adam, who managed to keep the fallen bikes between them.

"What'd you do? Sneak in through the attic while we were sleeping?" yelled Adam. A quarter century of sorrow, guilt, and rage emerged from down deep in the Jewish lawyer's soul, and he bashed headlights, wheel spokes, and engine casings in rhythm with his words.

"Did you just figure we didn't want him because he wasn't

perfect? Did you figure we wouldn't mind if you just took him out of our lives?"

Roman Loon ducked low between the Vincent's wheels and made a grab for Adam's foot, but Adam backed away, taunting:

"Thought you'd get away with it, didn't you? I mean, what crime gets solved after twenty-five years? That only happens in storybooks, right?" said Adam, approaching Roman's precious Laverda. "Now here's a pretty one," Adam said, raising his tire iron over the Day-Glo orange paint.

"No, no, not that one," screamed Roman Loon.

"So you like this bike," said Adam. "Well, in that case I'm just giving you an excuse to repaint it." With this he brought the tire iron crashing into the Laverda's gas tank with all his strength, putting a dent the size of a soccer ball in the beautiful European metalwork.

"You miserable son of a bitch," said Roman, very softly, staring at Adam, who stood triumphantly amid the mass of spoiled spokes. The kidnapper put the drill down and picked up a hydraulic jack from the floor. He came at Adam swinging it, the muscles in his burgling arms bulging, his face pulled back in a horrible grimace. Adam, who had exhausted his fury on the Laverda bashings, suddenly realized that Roman Loon was playing for keeps, and he was afraid. He tried to get out of the way as Roman drew closer. The wind from the jack brushed his nose, and Adam ducked behind Roman's grinding machine.

"I'm going to make you look like that fuel tank," Roman roared, his turn to feel hatred and fury. He wound up for another blow at the fleeing lawyer, twisting his shoulders and his waist so that the truck jack would go through Adam Steinberg as surely as a machete through a watermelon. Adam was pinned against Roman's tool rack now, and he ducked and weaved the slow but deadly orbit of the jack. The tool rack was of white Peg-Board, with specialty implements hung on bent hooks in neat rows. Keeping his eye on the maniac Loon, Adam reached above him and grabbed at the board. His hand closed around a huge screwdriver and he pulled it free and

hurled it at Roman's head. Roman ducked, and the screwdriver hit a 1960 G50 Matchless against the opposite wall. It
made a clanging sound as it slid across the valve cover, leaving
a hideous gash.

"Ha," said Adam Steinberg.

Roman turned quickly to see where the screwdriver had
landed, and at that moment Adam made a grab for the jack.
Gasoline from the insulted Laverda and oil from the other
machines was forming in a pool beneath Roman's feet. When
he saw Adam grabbing he spun and tugged back on the jack,
losing his balance on the slick beneath him. His eyes bulging,
his arms flailing in the air, Roman relinquished the truck lift to
Adam's squash grip and fell back, his head striking the edge of
the grinding table with a sickening thud.

Even though Roman Loon was by far the more formidable
male specimen, Adam Steinberg had prevailed by dint of sheer
luck. Roman's eyesight was blurred and he felt as if he was
going to vomit from the impact to his head. He was powerless
to do anything when Adam heaved against the big grinder and
tilted it over him.

"If I let go of this machine, it'll crush you like a Fabergé
egg," said Adam Steinberg.

"What do you want?" Roman managed, despite the fact
that he had never heard of a Fabergé egg.

"I want the truth about my son," said Adam.

"Your son," repeated Roman.

"I know that your son Scooter is my son Bernard," said
Adam. "He was stolen from my Bel Air house twenty-five
years ago."

"I don't know what you're talking about," said Roman
Loon one last time.

"Then you won't ever know anything again," said Adam,
tilting the machine another twenty degrees.

Roman Loon's head began to clear from the force of the
blow, and his fuzzy, whirling world was replaced by the focused image of Adam Steinberg and a slicing pain above his
ear. Roman was accustomed to dire straits, and he knew that
his only chance was to outwit his attacker.

"I bought him," lied Roman, releasing his breath and lying flat as an empty tire.

"You mean you purchased him?"

"My late wife couldn't have children," Roman lied again. "We wanted a boy more than anything."

"Why didn't you just adopt?" demanded Adam.

"We couldn't get the references, do you have any idea what it takes—"

"So you didn't kidnap him yourself?"

"Some gang, some people that I knew, they took him, I didn't even know where he was from, he was cheaper because of his, his, you know, fingers and toes." Watching Adam's pinched gray face, Roman knew that the lawyer believed him.

"Who were they, these people? What were their names?"

"I don't remember," said Roman, "it's so long ago."

Adam lowered the grinding machine again.

"I know they heard about him through some doctor in Beverly Hills," said Roman. "The doctor knew you, or knew your wife."

Adam was so stunned, he nearly dropped the machine on Roman's head. The cat burglar had recovered sufficiently to roll out of the way, however, and the machine went crashing to the floor with an enormous boom. A sweet, electrical smell filled the air.

"Your baby-gang people knew a doctor in Beverly Hills?"

"Or his nurse, or something," said Roman, climbing to his feet. "The word that I got was that the parents, I guess that's you, didn't want the kid."

Adam slumped against the fallen grinder and Roman rested against the Vincent Comet, holding a shop rag to his head.

"I know who this doctor is," said Adam.

"Yes," said Roman Loon.

"He's a handsome man, our son," said Adam.

"I know," said Roman Loon.

"He seems very intelligent."

"He's a genius," Roman said.

"He works in advertising," said Adam.

"I know," Roman Loon said again.

"When I tell the police you'll go to jail," said Adam Steinberg, straightening, his anger returning slowly as the enormity of what he had just been told sunk in.

"I love him," said Roman Loon. "My Marian lived and breathed for him. He wanted for nothing, we gave him all we had."

"My wife bore him," said Adam, spitting. "He's a part of me. You're going to rot in jail for this, and so is your baby gang."

"You can't tell him," said Roman, suddenly gaining height.

Adam picked up the electric drill where Roman had dropped it and squeezed the trigger switch to make it buzz.

"If you tell him I'm not his real father," Roman Loon said slowly, "I will tell him that you and your wife wanted to be rid of him."

"That's preposterous," said Adam Steinberg, paling.

"I'll also tell him that he can check with the FBI. I'll tell him that you, a big Los Angeles lawyer, if I remember correctly, did nothing at all to make sure he was found."

"There was nothing we could do," said Adam.

"Maybe true, maybe not, but I doubt he'll believe it when he sees your house. There were no TV spots, no ads taken out in magazines, no appeals from the police, no posters on trees and in supermarkets."

"How do you know we didn't do those things?" Adam asked.

"It's not me you have to convince," said Roman Loon. "It's the boy. If you tell him that I stole him, I'll tell him that you arranged the whole thing because a kid with extra fingers and toes didn't fit into your country-club world. If you make him hate me, I'll make him hate you more."

Adam Steinberg drove home to Bel Air slowly, his head whirling with thoughts of Scooter. He tried to imagine him as a little boy, all dirty from motorcycle grease, sitting on Roman's knee. He tried to imagine Roman's wife, and what she had looked like, and he thought, too, of his betrayal at the hands of his old friend from Yale. Guilt and frustration snowballed in his head, and gradually his thoughts turned to revenge. When he neared his law office Adam changed his mind and headed for home, knowing there was no way he could keep his mind on his work.

Sharon was surprised to see him home so early.

"Are you sick?" she asked.

"I'm fine," said lawyer Adam to the mother of his two children. "I took the morning off and went to Santa Barbara."

"You didn't," said Sharon.

"I went to meet the father of Mr. Loon."

"Oh, Adam," Sharon said.

"He's not our son, Sharon," Adam told her. "Apparently this type of malformation is more common than we thought. Our young Mr. Loon was conceived on a shore leave from a freighter off the Malay coast. His father was in the merchant marine."

Sharon sat down and started to cry. "I suppose," she sniffed, "I should be disappointed, but in a way I'm relieved. It all hurts so much. Poor Bernard. I hope he's doing well, wherever he is."

"I hope so too," said Adam, putting his arm around her shoulder.

"Was his father a nice man?"

"Very nice," said Adam. "Really a lovely man."

27

After a quarter century of pursuit, Niles Grosbeak was delirious with joy at the capture of Harlan Kowalski. The G-man knew that he was about to break the back of a heinous criminal cadre and he pushed Harlan hard for information about the rest of the gang. The orchid lover was shrewd, however, and not easily intimidated by his captor.

"I need the names and addresses of others in your gang," said Grosbeak, standing especially tall in a small white room with a green folding card table and a clock.

"Suck me," said Harlan Kowalski.

"I need the names and addresses of at least six people that work with you," said Grosbeak again.

"I raise orchids, I don't know what you're talking about."

"You raise orchids for a living?"

"Sure," said Harlan, adjusting the straps on his suspenders.

"I think you sell babies for a living," said Niles.

"Eat me," said Harlan. "I'm a flower breeder."

"You sure you don't sell dog food?" said Grosbeak.

"I don't know what you're talking about."

"I think you sold dog food to Melissa Midwhittle of Santa Ana, California, before you stole her child and then left him for pickup in a banana crate at San Pedro."

"When you got proof of all these things you think," said Harlan, studiously picking his nose, "then we'll talk."

At this Niles Grosbeak picked up the phone and arranged for Melissa Midwhittle and her baby to be brought to central California immediately by plane.

By 9 P.M. the same evening the parent of the banana bantling had viewed Harlan Kowalski in a lineup and identified him as the man who had sold her the doctored dog food.

"You have been identified as the man who stole the banana child," Grosbeak told Harlan as the other men in the lineup were led away.

"Can't be true," said Harlan sleepily. "Nobody saw nothing."

"Thank you," said Niles, with a smile. "I have just tape-recorded you telling me that nobody saw you stealing the baby."

"I didn't say that," said Harlan.

"You're going to jail, Harlan. You're never going to breathe free air again. I can help you, but only if you cooperate."

"Fuck off," said Harlan.

"Of course you may not spend much time at all in the slammer, since kidnapping is a capital offense," said Niles, running his fingers up and down his necktie and looking everywhere but at Harlan. "I'm going to be there when they turn on the juice," he said.

"What juice?"

"Oh, you know, after they've strapped you in the chair, and they've shaved your head, and your chest, and your arms and legs, and wired you up. They say that sometimes the wires don't make good contact and the flesh burns. One time, myself, I saw steam coming out of a fellow's ears. He was screaming the whole time, though, so I don't know exactly what he was feeling."

"I can't give you any names," said Harlan. "They'll kill me."

"I think you're right not to," said Grosbeak, rising and yawning. "You're going to die anyway, so why spill the beans on your friends? No doubt they're laughing all the way to the bank about this. Good night, Kowalski. It's been fun."

"I'll tell you about the kids," said Harlan slowly, "but I won't tell you about the gang."

Grosbeak's heart soared as he was given the first concrete evidence in twenty-five years that a ring actually existed. He kept the elation from his face, however, as he began to write down the names and dates of babies that Harlan remembered pinching and vending.

Once the FBI had a chance to track down the leads Kowalski had provided, Grosbeak released information to the press detailing the criminal's capture and also the names of the babies that had been recovered. A front-page newspaper article followed, which at Niles's behest suggested that not only had Harlan revealed victim information but had squealed on his confederates like the pig farmer he was. The article went on to announce that multiple arrests were expected any day. Grosbeak's strategy, of course, was to galvanize the baby gang, on whom he had really no leads whatsoever, into action and thence into error.

This news hit the papers two days after Harlan was captured and identified by Melissa Midwhittle. The leader of the baby gang read the news while breakfasting on fresh-squeezed orange juice and coffee in his Topanga Canyon home not far from Biji Steinberg's former flat.

The criminal had purchased the house eight years earlier, despite prognostications of bad fortune from earthquake-conscious financial investors, and had refurbished it in grand bachelor style. The southern side of the house sported floor-to-ceiling glass, and there was redwood-beam work, a Jacuzzi inside and one outside, and custom furniture made from cherry wood that the kidnapper had commissioned while on a trip to visit relatives in New Hampshire. The entire house was covered in white rugs, which the owner steam-cleaned compulsively with a machine he kept in the closet.

He had just raised a raisin English muffin to his mouth when the baby-gang leader saw Harlan's picture on the front page of the paper. He choked on a bit of crust and fruit and his hands turned suddenly sweaty. When he recovered enough to sip his juice, he read the article quickly. The ulcer that had been with him since Clea left him twinged mercilessly, and the kidnapper groaned and leapt to his feet. His serving maid, who had been giving the living-room furniture a once-over with a feather duster, saw him totter and ran to his aid.

"The phone," he said roughly, spitting crumbs.

The maid brought him a small cordless device made in Japan, and the baby-gang leader immediately dialed the number of his third-in-command. There was no answer. What the gang leader did not know was that Harlan's assistant was already on his way to Mexico with a sackful of cash and a valuable collection of ancient Greek coins hidden in his socks.

The gang leader's next call was to Clea at her Beverly Hills home. Her husband, Adam Steinberg's betrayer and former college classmate, answered the phone. The baby-gang leader identified himself as the owner of the drapery cleaning service that the doctor's wife had ordered and the medico handed Clea the phone without remark.

"It's me," said the baby-gang leader.

"I've already had them cleaned this summer, thank you, anyway," she said, and hung up.

Cursing, the baby-gang leader called again. Clea let the phone ring twice and then answered.

"Don't hang up," he said. "This is important."

"You don't have anything important to say to me," she replied, starting to hang up again.

"You're about to be arrested and spend the rest of your life in jail," the baby-gang leader shouted into the mouthpiece.

Clea heard his voice just before the receiver met the cradle. She picked the phone up again. "What are you talking about?" she asked.

"Go look at the front page of the L.A. *Times*," said the baby-gang leader. "I'll hold."

When Clea saw Harlan's picture she turned it quickly toward her ample chest and picked up the phone again.

"My God," she said. "Where are you calling from?"

"My house," he said.

"That means that they don't know about us yet or we would have been arrested already."

"The article says different," said her ex-husband.

"They're just trying to flush us out," said Clea. "We need to talk."

"As soon as your husband sees the paper, that's going to be difficult."

"He doesn't know who Harlan is, but you're right, we must meet tonight. Do you know Carillo Beach?"

"Of course," snorted the chairman of the board of kidnapping operations.

"I'll meet you there at midnight. I'll give my husband a sleeping pill."

"You can't do that," said the baby-gang leader, "he's a doctor."

"I'll put him to sleep somehow," she said. "You know I can."

"I know you can," the baby-gang leader said with a sigh.

Leo Carillo State Beach lies up the California coast from Malibu, past Zuma, but not as far as the navy bases at Oxnard. It is a small beach, accessible only by curving, sometimes windblown, stretches of highway, and features stone formations that give it fine character. Because it is a drive from downtown, it is less jammed in the summertime than the beaches farther south.

Clea left her Beverly Hills home at quarter to eleven in order to assure herself ample setup time for the meeting with her former husband. She took with her a Smith & Wesson Airweight revolver that she had purchased during the years she spent in association with the baby gang. The gun was small and light and did not make a bulge in her handbag. The moon was nearly full, and shadows from the canyon lands gave the road in front of her car a ghostly feel. Clea left the windows open in her car, and though she had liberally doused herself in expensive French perfume, she could just make out the smell of the brine. When she reached the beach she drove back and forth for several miles on either side of the entrance. She wanted to be sure there were no young couples necking on the beach and no police cars cruising. At ten minutes to twelve she parked her car by one end of the beach lot and lit a cigarette. While she smoked it she turned on the radio to get the latest on the hunt for the baby gang, but there was a great deal of static and she could make out nothing clearly.

At precisely midnight Clea took off her shoes, left her car, and went carefully down to the sea. She checked the revolver nervously, then closed her handbag and sat listening to the lapping of the waves. Soon she heard the familiar low growl of her ex-husband's Ferrari. When he met her on the beach moments later, his face was drawn and his eyes were wild.

"This is it," he giggled. "The jig is up, as they say."

"He won't talk," said Clea. "He's been with you too long."

"No, no," said the master napper, "you don't understand. He's already singing like a canary. They've even tracked some of the kids. They're taking them away from perfectly good families and giving them back to boozing, starving perverts. Some of them are grown up already!"

"Do you know for a fact that he's told them your name?" asked Clea.

"I don't know any facts at all," said the baby-gang leader.

"But the police haven't called?"

"Nobody calls, parrot dung, parrot dung, what's this green stuff on my tongue?" sang the baby-gang leader, starting to shake, boogie, and rhumba all over the beach.

"What are you doing?" said Clea in disgust.

"I'm dancing in the moonlight," the man giggled again.

"You're cracking up, aren't you? Why don't you just run somewhere, leave the country or something?"

"Where can I go, where can I go, where can I go that the wind don't blow?"

"I've got a place," said Clea, thinking of how close she was to losing everything she had. "Where I'm going to send you it's very still. Where I'm going to send you there's no wind at all."

The baby-gang leader stopped moving and stared at the gun.

"You wouldn't," he said.

"If they catch you," she said, "you'll tell them about me.

You'll tell them about my husband and the leads and the babies. I know you will."

"I won't say anything," the baby-gang leader said, waving and moving toward the muzzle of the Smith & Wesson. "You know I won't."

"I know you will," said Clea, shooting him in the heart.

In the movies and on television, when people are shot they die instantly, either closing their eyes like a sleeper or staring dully at the camera. The baby-gang leader did neither. The bullet only seemed to increase the tempo of his steps, and although the blood in his mouth kept him from singing, he put out his arms as if he wanted Clea for a partner. When she saw this she shot him again in the forehead, and finally his dance was done.

28

The screenwriter who had worked on the banana-bantling script had stayed as close to the truth as he could without having to pay Melissa Midwhittle more than a token sum for story rights. In the film the kidnappers were crazed Cuban drug runners, and the infant's parents were a Minneapolis stockbroker and his deaf-mute wife. The discovery of the infant on the docks in a banana crate was accurate, however, and with Scooter's banana billboards in place all over Los Angeles, the constantly breaking news piqued the interest of moviegoers everywhere. In order to open the show while the subject was still current, Murray Feldman stepped up production and the filming and editing were complete the day after the baby-gang leader was killed.

Biji had remained in residence with Reno since Murray evicted her from her Malibu apartment, but she had also continued her clandestine meetings with Scooter. Even though she knew it made her look whorish, when the filming was over she told Reno they were too.

"You just stayed with me for the film?" said the big black man. "Baby, I wouldn't have believed it about you."

"Look, Reno," she said, "I didn't sleep with you to get the part. I already had the part."

"Then why did you stay?" he asked, simultaneously fearing the truth and needing to hear it.

"I stayed because I cared for you, because I enjoyed being with you, and because Murray kicked me out of my apartment," said Biji.

"You could have gotten your own place anytime," said Reno. "You're a rich woman lady now. This has to do with Scooter Loon, doesn't it? You moving in with him?"

"I really don't know," said Biji.

"If you're lying to me, girl, I'll take your pants down right here."

Even though she didn't like being called "girl," and liked the idea of him threatening her with a spanking even less, Biji had to laugh at Reno Raven's choice of words.

"I need to live my own life for a while, Reno," said Biji, standing on her tiptoes just to kiss him on the neck.

He responded by cupping her buttocks with his giant hands, looping his thumbs up and inside her waist and tugging at her slacks.

"Just one last taste of you," he said.

"Oh, Reno," said Biji.

"I guess that means I've had it," the big man said sadly. "I should have known you were too good to be true."

Biji was being less than completely honest with her costar, but this was out of a desire to spare his feelings. Things had escalated a great deal in the months she had spent with Scooter, and although he had not become her lover, he had quickly become her best friend.

"I want to get a dog," Biji announced to the adman one day as they strolled around the Westwood section of Los Angeles, near the University of California.

"Ah," said Scooter.

"A big dog," she said. "A Briard or a Bouvier des Flandres."

"A Briard I know," he said, "big and hairy. The other I haven't heard of."

"Something that Scooter Loon doesn't know!" said Biji in mock horror, holding her hand to her mouth.

"It's rare," said Scooter, "but it happens."

"The Bouvier is another big guard dog," she said.

"I never would have guessed," said Scooter. "Why do you want a dog, anyway?"

The truth of the matter was that Biji really didn't want a dog, but she felt it was a convenient way to raise the issue of where she was to live. She figured that the discussion would soon turn to where she might keep the dog, and she wanted to talk to Scooter about her feelings without upsetting him.

"For protection," she said. "Since I don't have Reno Raven to do the job anymore."

For a moment Scooter was stunned, but he recovered himself quickly. "Protection from whom?" he laughed. "Reporters?"

"I just think it would be good to have one," said Biji. "Or maybe a Borzoi, you know, a Russian wolfhound. That would keep people away."

"Is that what you want to do?" Scooter said gently, stopping and turning suddenly to face her. "Do you want to keep people away?"

"For a while," she said.

"And what would you do with the dog when you went out to dinner, or when you were working, or out on dates?" he said.

"I'd take it along."

"You would take a Russian wolfhound out to dinner?" said Scooter. "I see. And when you had to leave it at home?"

"I'd leave it," Biji replied.

"But where's home?" said Scooter. "I mean that's really the point, isn't it?"

"I hate you sometimes," said Biji.

"Well, I think you should know something very important," said Scooter.

"What?"

"I'm allergic to dogs."

Even though Scooter was crying out to be with Biji, and wanted her desperately to move into his sagebrush apartment in Santa Monica, there was a conservative reluctance to life and sex with Biji that Scooter had never felt with Faranak. If they were going to live together, he knew she was going to have to talk him into it.

Biji, on the other hand, was just coming to terms with the role of men in her life. Aside from a multitude of boyfriends with whom she had been intimate but never truly close, there had only been four men in Biji's life before Scooter. The first was her father, with whom her relationship was distant and strained. The second was her mother's doctor, who had cut her and made her forever barren. The third was Murray Feldman, who had used her without shame, and the fourth was Reno Raven, whom she had definitely thought she loved until she met Scooter Loon. Her feelings toward Scooter were undeniable and strong, but perhaps because he was so much like her, she remained a little bit afraid of what he could come to mean to her. Biji saw what her parents had and didn't want it, but she was not old enough to realize that her life could be any way she wanted it.

"You couldn't live with my dog, then?" asked Biji.

"What dog? You don't even have a dog."

"Yes, but if I got one, you couldn't live with it?"

"I don't really think I could," said Scooter. "You wouldn't love me nearly so much with my eyes all swollen and my nose going drip, drip."

"You said 'love,'" said Biji Steinberg.

"Mmm," said Scooter Loon.

"I think I have to live at home for a while," said Biji, suddenly. "I think I need some time to think about things, some time to be with my parents."

Scooter was both disappointed and relieved. "I think I understand," he said. "Maybe a little time to put things with Reno into perspective."

Biji had been sure that Scooter would reject her, and when he didn't she was suddenly and terribly sure that she really did love him.

"Can we go to your place for a while?" she said, squeezing his hand. "I feel like sniffing some sagebrush."

The motorcycle ride from Westwood to Santa Monica was perhaps the most tense of Scooter's life. Besides the prospect of what he knew was about to happen, even a truck bumper, even a dead goat and a dead rider seemed like tame stuff. When they reached Scooter Loon's apartment building, Scooter parked his bike in the underground garage and locked both helmets to it. Without saying a word, he put his arm around Biji and led her upstairs.

While his sister stood silhouetted against the falling sun, Scooter watched from the open kitchen and uncorked a bottle of wine.

"I know you like it sweet," he said, marveling at the perfection of Biji. She wore white pants that stopped at the bottom of her muscular calves and a leotard top that showed how cold the ride had been. "This is a German Auslese. It's a little like the Château d'Yquem that Reno buys you."

"Who taught you about wine?" asked Biji, turning and stretching her arms above her head.

"Somebody I once knew," he said.

"The Persian girl, wasn't it?"

Scooter just smiled. He walked closer to her, holding both wineglasses, and when he handed her one their fingers touched. She took the glass.

"I love the smell in here," she said. "It's like the desert."

Scooter put one arm around her firm back and drew her to him. He took a sip of wine and let his lower lip get soaked.

"Taste," he said.

She put her own glass on the windowsill, put her hands behind his head, and drew him softly to her. Eyes open and locked with his, she licked the sweet drop from him.

When she had taken all the wine from the cleft above his chin, she opened her mouth and they melted together.

"Wait," he said. "Now let me." This time he raised his glass to her lips, and she took a sip and let the wine dribble down her throat. He bent to put the glass down beside hers, and then came up slowly, beginning at the depression that marked the top of her collarbone and licking all the way up and over the curve of her chin to her lips. He had expected her skin to be smooth and cool, but she was on fire for him. Her hands twined and untwined in his hair, and her breathing grew rough.

They remained standing in front of the window that looked out over the ocean and the palms. His kisses left her mouth and dropped lower, down to the swell of the tops of her breasts. He hooked his hands over the straps of her leotard and lowered it gently, taking her nipples in his mouth and making them rise. Biji's hands ran lower, too, leaving his head for his neck and then moving inside his shirt, unbuttoning and tearing until his chest was against hers.

They undressed each other in stages, a sleeve here, a leg there, until they were naked and pressed tight. Scooter's desire was mighty, but not as great as his joy in simply holding the woman he wanted to be with forever. Biji, too, abandoned herself to the moment. Forgetting the schemes and the risks, she clutched him to her and drew him to the floor.

They began together beneath the living-room window, but their grappling and grasping was so fierce that they ended up with Biji's auburn hair rubbing hard against the sliding door that led to Scooter's terrace. With the light coming in on her mussed tight curls and her half-closed eyes, Scooter saw how vulnerable she was, and what her tough act cost her. When at last he parted her smooth brown thighs and entered her, Biji felt the sweetest wave, and Scooter felt like he was coming home.

The next morning Scooter dropped Biji in Bel Air on his way to work. Lawyer Adam was at the office, but Sharon Steinberg was home.

"I've left Reno Raven," Biji told her mother.

Sharon could barely conceal her joy.

"I've been dating Scooter Loon," she said.

"The boy who makes up those ads for you," said Sharon, "the boy with the extra toe."

"I didn't think you noticed things like that," said Biji with a smile. "Things are good between us, but I don't want to move right in with him. I want to be at home with you and Dad for a while. I want to take it slow."

"It's always good to take it slow." Sharon nodded solemnly.

29

The press gave front-page attention to the shooting death of the baby-gang leader, identifying the murder victim as a prominent Los Angeles playboy who had invested heavily in real estate. The article noted that the man's neighbors complained often about his loud, sexually oriented parties, and added that the police were investigating the strong possibility that the dirty deed had been committed by a spurned lover.

When Harlan Kowalski read of his boss's death, he immediately summoned Special Agent Grosbeak with a message that he was ready to talk.

"You know that you've given me zero so far," Grosbeak told him from the doorway to his cell.

"Get me out of here," said Harlan. "Take me someplace we can talk."

Niles led Grosbeak back to the interrogation room with the green card table.

"I don't want to go to the chair," said Kowalski.

"Out of my hands," said Niles, spreading his hands. "The names and addresses of your victims helped, but some of them were untraceable, and the parents are all screaming for your blood. There may not be much I can do."

"I can give you the leader," said Harlan.

"How do I know there is one?" asked Grosbeak.

"You've gone through all my computer files," said Harlan. "I know you have. Did you notice the word *Overlord* in the programs?"

Grosbeak had indeed sent a team in to Kowalski's Morro Bay house the day the big man had been captured and already had transcripts of Harlan's work on his desk. The "Overlord" reference had already caught his attention.

"I'm listening," said Niles.

"I can tell you who 'Overlord' is, but you have to give me something in return."

"Reduced sentence," said the G-man, who had already arranged the plea bargain with a judge. "No chair, twenty years max, you're out on parole in seven."

"You might not like what you hear," said Harlan. "I mean you might not want to know."

"Don't play games with me, flower man," said Grosbeak. "I need the name. Give me the name."

"So it's a deal? It doesn't matter who he is, you want to know?" The pig farmer stuck out his hand.

Grosbeak took the outstretched palm with evident distaste. "It's a deal, Kowalski," he said. "But if you feed me a line, I'll bury you so deep daylight can't find you."

Harlan reached into the pocket of his blue prison work shirt and pulled out the article about the baby-gang leader's death.

"Here's your man," Harlan said with a smile. "I guess you won't be talking to him."

The baby-gang leader left behind a quiet trail of moderate investments in strip malls around California. These had been designed to give him a cover, something to explain his lavish life-style and debauched parties, something to satisfy nosy friends and tax officials. While the proceeds from this portfolio made him rich by most people's standards, they were but a small fraction of his income from the sale of kidnapped children.

Niles Grosbeak, crook catcher extraordinaire, threw himself into an investigation of the baby-gang leader the likes of which the criminal element had rarely seen. Grosbeak went to the dead man's house, sat in the dead man's chair, took in the view from the dead man's porch, read the dead man's mail, and went through every single article of clothing in the dead man's closets. Assisted by a forensics team, he also visited the Carillo

Beach murder site and took back with him to San Francisco a vague plaster impression of former nurse Clea's footprint.

Feeling that he was indeed and at last truly on the trail of his nemesis, Special Agent Grosbeak spent the better part of a week reconstructing an account of the dead man's life, including his one and only marriage to a woman now living in Beverly Hills.

Clea's new last name, given to her by the doctor who had butchered Biji, rang no prompt bell in Grosbeak's head. It had been nearly a quarter of a century since the bony man had quizzed the doctor in the study of Adam Steinberg's Bel Air home, and there had been many names to remember since then, including most recently that of Melissa Midwhittle, the very mention of whom brought a blush to Niles's cheeks. So Niles ran a computer cross-check, indexing names and addresses in the files he had been so diligently updating over the years. He sat in front of the amber screen at his northern California headquarters and watched as the tiny electronic cursor scanned the years of data for a clue. It was several moments before the screen revealed the tie-in to the case of Steinberg, Bernard.

The theft of Scooter Loon was an abomination that lived with Niles every day. Although only one of many, the case of little malformed Bernard stuck out in Niles's mind, not only because the child had been taken from a family of wealth and power, but because if any baby should have been able to be traced, Grosbeak thought, little Bernie Steinberg was that baby. His failure to come up with a lead on the misfingered boy had embarrassed him beyond measure, and he had never forgotten the feeling. When he saw Clea's name he remembered the doctor and was ashamed that it had taken the computer to remind him.

Grosbeak returned at once to the central coast for another meeting with Harlan Kowalski.

"I don't know no Steinberg," said Harlan. "We don't take kids from Bel Air, there's a security patrol there. Doesn't matter where the kid's from, anyway. The buyers don't even want to know. Price's the same, why chance it?"

"The challenge. The same reason you took the banana kid from a house full of dogs. I know you, Kowalski, I know how you think. You like a challenge, the risk."

"You don't know shit," said Harlan.

"Then how come you're in jail?" said Special Agent Niles Grosbeak.

"I don't know nothing about no Steinberg kid. I'd tell you, wouldn't I? I already told you everything."

Harlan was telling the truth. He had never been privy to the theft of little Bernard, a crime that had been arranged by his boss and committed by Roman Loon.

"Ask that cold bitch Clea," he told Grosbeak. "She knew everything her old man was into. If he had anything to do with it, she'll know for sure."

Acting on this information, Niles had the doctor and his wife put under surveillance by the Los Angeles office of the FBI, members of which were already interested in Clea in connection with the baby-gang leader's violent death.

Despite the fact that she had overlooked one footprint, Clea had been extremely attentive to covering her trail. She had taken a broom with her in the trunk of her car and had swept the tire tracks off of the surface of the beach parking lot. She had even gone through the car wash twice with her Mercedes and had thrown the shoes she wore at the scene away in a Dumpster behind a sushi bar near the coast. Clea expected to be questioned in connection with the baby-gang leader's murder, and she thought she was ready for anything.

When the doctor heard of the shooting death of his wife's former husband, he totally lost his composure.

"First there are all these newspaper articles about kidnappers," he wailed, "and now somebody's killed your ex-husband. You can be sure they'll be here to ask you questions."

"I haven't seen the man in years," Clea told him. "Anyway, you know he ran with a nasty bunch. I'm sure they have plenty of suspects."

"And I'm sure you're one of them," the gynecologist interrupted. "What do we do if the police show up here? What if they put us together with this gang? What if whoever killed him comes after us next?"

"Oh stop whining like a sick horse," said Clea. "I'm sure the gang in the paper had nothing to do with my ex, and even if it did, it has nothing to do with us."

"I wouldn't exactly say nothing," said the doctor. "What about the Steinberg boy?"

"One baby out of many, years and years ago," said Clea. "And besides, you didn't kidnap him, what're you worried about?"

"They could trace it back," said the doctor, holding his head in his hands. "They could connect it to me because I know Adam Steinberg."

"Who said anything about Adam Steinberg?" said Clea. "Why do you even bring up his name?"

30

Sometimes the people who have the most in life are seized with the fear that they have the least. This fear comes not so much from an objective sense of spiritual scale but rather from a paroxysm of doubt, a sudden worry that they have just spent the bulk of their life completely missing the point. The life-styles that others around them have chosen all at once appear somehow meatier, their own lives a thin broth by contrast. Some people refer to this change of vision as a mid-life crisis. Others refer to it as being born again. Yet others call it "finally growing up."

At the age of fifty Adam Steinberg was suddenly seized by a host of regrets, all catalyzed by his meeting with the father of his son. He began to wonder whether the fancy house and sporty cars were worth it, and for days he moaned alone in his office, his hands on his ears, as he thought of the son he had lost and the daughter he still didn't know. There was, of course, no way to redo his life wearing a different suit with a different heart stapled to the sleeve. What Adam was left with, after the frustration and the tears had come and gone, was the desire for revenge. Having everything except what he had come to think was the only thing that mattered, Adam was suddenly willing to risk losing it all.

Southern California, from the desert to the coast, retains at least one characteristic of the Old West: It is a land of guns. Roman Loon had many guns, Clea had the one she needed, and Adam Steinberg, the high forehead of the law, had one too.

He kept it in the bottom right-hand drawer of his desk, and it was a serious piece, manufactured in Belgium by some of the finest arms manufacturers in the world. It was more potent than Clea's gun, but not so overwhelming as Niles Grosbeak's cannon, which was capable of going well into the engine block of a fleeing car.

Adam was pretty handy with his gun, taking it once a month to the police range and shooting a tight, accurate pattern on paper while officers he knew watched approvingly. Now the day had come, Adam knew, for him to fire his gun into the heart of his old Yale buddy.

He had talked little with the doctor since confronting him with Biji's confession. At that time the doctor had explained to Adam and his wife how their daughter had come to him in the final stages, bleeding and in danger of losing her life and demanding from him absolute professional confidence. He had done the best he could for her, the gynecologist told the Bel Air couple, but it was tragically true that she would never be able to bear children. When Sharon began to rant and rave and threaten a lawsuit, the doctor had mildly explained that much as he valued the Steinbergs' friendship, his first allegiance and responsibility was to his patients. Where darling Biji was concerned, he said, he had done the only thing he could do.

Now it was time for Adam Steinberg to do the same.

It was evening before Niles Grosbeak arrived at the home of the man who had mangled Biji and orchestrated the theft of her brother. The house was a generous, sprawling, stone affair, unusual in a subtropical area where wood and shingle were the rule. FBI men were in stakeout positions at either end of the street and in the alley behind Clea's kitchen. They were also in a spare bedroom of the house across the street, having secured the owner's permission. Niles checked in with his men at the second-story observation post and was on his way across the street just as Adam Steinberg arrived, toting a briefcase that no one could know contained a pistol. Clea met Adam at the door and invited him into the living room. Using recording devices planted on the frames of expensive pictures, the agents listened to the doctor offer Adam a drink and they heard Adam decline. It was at this moment that Niles himself rang the bell.

Had Special Agent Grosbeak appeared five minutes later, the outcome of his investigations might have turned out very differently. The FBI would doubtless have heard Adam accuse the doctor of aiding in the kidnapping of his son, Bernard. Grosbeak would have wanted to know where Adam got his information, and Roman Loon's involvement in the case would, perforce, have emerged.

As it happened Niles Grosbeak appeared before Adam could open his briefcase and withdraw his gun. This was good for Adam, who would surely have been promptly jumped by a variety of active and well-trained young agents eager to wrestle him to the ground and disarm him.

"FBI, sir," said Niles Grosbeak, flashing his badge as the doctor opened the door. "I'd like to ask you a few questions."

"What's this about?" said the gynecologist.

"Surely you were expecting a visit after you read of the shooting death of your wife's former husband," Niles replied. "And while we're at it, I'd like to talk to you about the disappearance, many years ago, of an infant boy named Bernard Steinberg."

"My son," said Adam Steinberg, appearing from behind the door, tanned and well dressed.

In the quarter century following their last meeting, both Adam and Niles had changed less than one might imagine. True, Adam was softer and grayer of flesh, while Niles had become harder and more birdlike, but they were at heart the same men. Neither had been ravaged by any untoward sickness or loss, and when Adam spoke Special Agent Grosbeak knew at once who he was.

"Nice to see you again, Mr. Steinberg." Grosbeak smiled slightly. "How's life in Bel Air?"

"I want to stay and hear this," said Adam.

Grosbeak considered a minute. "I'm afraid that won't be possible, sir," he said. "This is a government investigation."

"It's a government investigation into the theft of my son,"

shouted Adam, waving his weapon-laden briefcase in the air.
"I know I have the right to hear this."

Although Grosbeak knew that Adam did not have that
right, he was loath to be distracted from his questioning by a
confrontation with the well-connected attorney.

"Very well, Mr. Steinberg," he said. "But only if you promise not to interfere."

Adam acquiesced with a tilt of his head.

"This is the way I see it," the G-man told Clea after they
were all comfortably seated in the garishly decorated living
room. "Mr. Harlan Kowalski, a kidnapping suspect now in
our custody, has named your ex-husband as the leader of a
gang of men who for the past thirty years have been abducting
young children and selling them for a profit. Mr. Kowalski
also claims that, during the years you were married to his
leader, you were privy to all the operations of the gang."

"I'm shocked," interrupted the doctor.

"I also have in my possession," Grosbeak continued plac-
idly, "the mold of a shoe made at Leo Carillo State Beach
where your former husband was cruelly gunned down. The
shoe is a size seven. What size is your shoe, ma'am?" said
Grosbeak.

"I really don't see what this has to do with my—" Adam
Steinberg began.

Niles Grosbeak held up his hand.

"At the time that Mr. Steinberg's infant son, Bernard, was
taken," Grosbeak said, turning to the doctor, "was not your
wife working for you as a nurse?"

"She was," replied the doctor.

"And was she aware that Sharon Steinberg gave birth to a
boy with a certain birth defect?" asked the government agent.

At this point the doctor, who deep down was a spineless
man, began to fear that the woman to whom he was still so
fearfully physically addicted might be dragging him into something bigger than he had imagined. He heard Niles insinuate
that his wife was a murderess, and looking at her frigid glare
and stiff position, he thought the agent might be right. In his

warped scheme of values, kidnapping and impromptu surgery
might be acceptable, but a bullet in the brain was not.

"I'm sure she was," said the doctor, his face starting to
twitch. "And now that you explain it this way, I can only
surmise that all the time she was my nurse she was in fact
working for a gang of infant thieves—"

Clea had been sitting silently through the interrogation, secure in the assumption that Grosbeak was just fishing. When
her husband suddenly turned on her, she lost her composure
utterly.

"Shut up, shut up, shut up," she screamed.

"I cannot tell you how used this makes me feel," the gynecologist said to Niles Grosbeak.

"You were the one who told me they didn't want the child,"
ranted Clea. "You were the one who said that the baby had to
end up far, far from here!"

"May I see your foot?" Niles asked her.

Adam Steinberg, who had been listening with growing
amazement to Grosbeak's reconstruction of the crime, whirled
to face the doctor.

"You're going to die," he said, grabbing for the briefcase
that contained his Browning.

At that moment Clea opened a small white leather purse
that had been sitting on her lap and pulled out the Smith &
Wesson Airweight. She trained the bobbing nose on Grosbeak,
who sat serene as sand.

"Now listen," she said. "I'm going to walk out of here, and
you're going to come with me as my hostage."

"I'm afraid I can't do that," said Niles. "It wouldn't be
dignified, at my age, to have a woman half my size take me
prisoner."

"A woman with a gun," said Clea.

At this moment the doctor, who had been watching his wife
carefully, made a move in her direction.

"Clea," he said. "There's no point—"

She turned to face him and cocked the hammer back. At
this Niles Grosbeak dropped to the floor, and moving his old
body in the manner of some ground grouse, whipped his frame

against the chair, sending Clea pitching forward. The gun went off with a loud report, causing a small rain of plaster from the wall above lawyer Adam. Grosbeak took the woman's wrist in one gaunt hand and with the other withdrew his enormous magnum and placed it against Clea's nose. Adam Steinberg relaxed his grip on his briefcase and pushed it away.

"I'm sure my lab will have an interesting time with this," Grosbeak said, relieving her of the Smith & Wesson.

Clea spat and caught the G-man on the cheek. In return he pushed her head down hard against the coffee table, bone to glass. The doctor slumped to the floor.

"My only regret," Special Agent Grosbeak said to Adam Steinberg, as a troop of government agents suddenly stormed into the room, "is that I don't think I can find your boy. The only man who might know where he ended up is dead. I can't even tell you if the child is alive."

Adam Steinberg, still overwhelmed by the marching beat of his heart, could not think of anything to say. He just took long, unsteady breaths, first one, then another, and thought of Scooter Loon.

31

If the prerequisites to a box-office smash were known and defined, no film would ever flop. In fact, a successful movie, just like a successful life, is the result of opportunity, talent, luck, and timing. No two movies, just like no two lives, ever succeed for precisely the same reasons. Biji Steinberg's first film owed its triumph to the advertising genius of Scooter Loon, the serendipitous appearance of sensational kidnapping press, the draw of Reno Raven, and the talent of the new performer. This wonderful, magical concatenation of ingredients set new box-office records for the production and rocketed the slender, auburn-haired girl with the mismatched eyes to overnight national acclaim. In the public eye Biji Steinberg was not an insular young girl from Bel Air who loved a man she did not know was her brother. To her fans Biji was Lee Frisk, graceful and elegant on the arm of Reno Raven, with a face that melted hearts and a figure that nearly caused them to burst.

Biji's sudden fame did much to take her mind off the strange revelations of the previous week. Even though she was frantically busy with photo shoots, parties, and interviews, it still astounded her to find that she had once had a brother and that the child had been kidnapped. The young actress found it incredible that her parents and all their close friends could have kept that fact from her for twenty-one years.

"I can't imagine why you never told me," said Biji early one evening, staring over the kitchen counter at her mother's tear-stained face and noticing how very old Sharon looked.

"It was something that happened long before you were born," said Sharon.

"But good God, Mother, it's a serious thing! How many

people have children stolen away from them by a gang of kid-nappers?"

"We didn't know it was a gang of kidnappers," said Sharon. "We didn't know anything back then."

"But wasn't there an investigation, wasn't it in the newspapers?"

"We didn't want to make a fuss, we didn't—"

"Make a fuss?" said Biji. "You lost a son and you didn't want to make a fuss!"

"Your father was afraid that it would get little Bernie killed, or that he was already in a foreign country or something . . ." Sharon sobbed.

"But why didn't he do something on the sly?" said Biji. "Dad knows all the cops, I just don't understand. And your doctor, the bastard that cut me up. The same guy that's known Dad since college . . ." said Biji.

"He's in jail," said Sharon, "and his wife's going to be executed for murder, so you see in the end people do get what they deserve."

"Somehow there's no balance here," said Biji, turning to leave. "You didn't get your son back, and I never knew my brother. How could that one man have taken so much away from me?"

After Biji had gone upstairs to dress, Adam appeared in the kitchen.

"Sooner or later you have to speak to her," said Sharon, wiping the tears from her face with a napkin. "We have to stop thinking about Bernard. Look at our daughter, in the movies, in the papers, on TV. She's famous, Adam."

"She's the one not talking to me."

"She thinks you did something wrong, she doesn't understand . . ."

"I'll talk to her tonight."

"You can't," said Sharon, "she's going out."

"With the black actor?"

"No, she doesn't see him anymore," said Sharon.

"What are you talking about? I just saw them on the television together, holding hands."

"That's for the fans," said Sharon, smiling sadly. "Honestly, Adam, you're so old-fashioned. She's going out with the boy-friend."

"Another *schwartze*?"

"The advertising boy, that Scooter Loon that you thought . . ."

Adam froze.

"What?" he said.

"She's been seeing that Scooter Loon," said Sharon.

"She's been seeing Scooter Loon?"

"I'm sure I mentioned it."

"For how long?" said Adam.

"I guess it's been going on for a while now, ever since she moved out from Raven's house, even before, I think."

"She's already had a date with him?"

"I think it's beyond the dating stage."

"Beyond the dating stage."

"I think the boy's father is taking them both out to dinner tonight."

"His father!" screamed Adam Steinberg, every nerve in his body coming to attention.

At that moment the Steinberg's doorbell sounded. Adam seemed unable to move, so Sharon pushed past him and, dabbing at her eyes, opened the door to reveal Roman and Scooter Loon.

It seemed to Adam as if the world were progressing in slow motion. Roman Loon's pupils were the size of bowling balls, and his arms were shaking.

"She's almost ready, Scooter," said Sharon with a smile. "Why don't we go and get her?"

"This is my father, Roman Loon," said Bernard Steinberg, moving out of the way so his mother could shake hands with the man who so many years ago had snuck past her with a baby on his back.

Sharon shook Roman's hand and then led Scooter to wait for Biji.

"Why didn't you tell me about this?" the cat burglar hissed as soon as he and Adam were alone.

"I didn't know," Adam hissed back.

"Well, what the hell are we going to do about it?" said Roman.

Just then Biji appeared behind her father at the foot of the stairs. She wore a low-cut red silk dress that revealed an abundant cleavage. Roman looked at her and swallowed hard.

"I know my daughter," Adam whispered, his face very close to Roman Loon's. "She doesn't stay with anyone very long, she's married to her career. We'll just have to wait for this to blow over."

Roman Loon looked about the house he hadn't seen for so very long. Everything looked different with the lights on.

32

Even though Roman had long ago moved on to wrenching on motorcycles he still entertained fantasies of London rooftop hopping and of bringing home the big score. Many times when he was alone, fiddling with a carburetor or aligning a wheel, he would see himself enjoying the warm company of fellow thieves in the satisfying aftermath of a successful heist. What he enjoyed most about belonging to his fantastical underworld cadre was the thieves code of honor. He was certainly a crook, but in his own way Roman Loon was a very moral man.

The dinner with Biji and Scooter went off without a hitch because Biji had so much to say. She liked Roman and felt more comfortable sharing her career goals with him than she did sharing them with Adam Steinberg. Her openness with Roman allowed him to sit with his chin in his cupped hand and stare at her for an hour and a half without uttering a word. The waiter had to pry Roman's menu choice from him, and when it came Roman didn't eat. Scooter noticed, but he didn't mind. He found Biji transfixing too.

The dinner came to an end when Biji and Scooter announced that they had to go to a screening. It was important for Biji's career, she said, and Scooter felt that he should be there, too, to represent his agency. Roman decided to drive back to Santa Barbara instead of spending the night in L.A.

"Come up and see me tomorrow," said Roman as they parted outside the restaurant, which Biji had wanted to try because it was supposed to be a social hot spot.

"I'd love to," said Scooter. "But Biji and I have plans. We're taking a ride."

"Ride up the coast and come see me," said Roman.

"We were going to head for the mountains, maybe stay overnight someplace."

Roman winced at the mention of nocturnal intimacy. He was growing surer and surer all the time that despite whatever respect his imaginary British confederates might have had for his rooftop prowess, they would never have approved of incest.

"You could find a place up by me, with a view of the ocean. You could even stay with me, at the house."

Biji heard the pleading in Roman's voice and found it odd. It wasn't like Roman to sound so unsure of himself, and she gave Scooter a nudge with her elbow.

"There are some great ranches around there," she said.

Scooter looked at her in surprise.

"So then you'll come?" said Roman.

"We'll come," said Biji. Before Scooter could protest she locked her arm in his and propelled him away. When they were a few feet from Roman, she turned and waved.

Roman drove all the way back to Santa Barbara along the coast at night. He barely noticed the road. His mind was a fantasy machine. The first product was the image of his adopted son in bed with Biji Steinberg. This image was very graphic because Roman Loon was a man of great imagination. Near the spot along the Pacific Coast Highway where Clea shot her husband in cold blood, Roman became so disturbed that he nearly drove off the road and plunged into the sea.

His next pang of conscience came as he was nearing the small strip of houses north of Ventura known as La Conchita. He looked to the winking lights of an offshore oil-drilling platform and saw Marian's face hovering out over the water, complexion pale in the moonlight. She had her hand to her mouth in horror.

Next he saw himself being hunted down by his band of thieves and strung up by the neck from the hands of Big Ben, the crowds below the bell tower pointing at him and calling him an abomination before God.

Waiting for Scooter and Biji the next day was harder on Roman's nervous system than any flight from the law had ever been. It was harder than keeping Scooter quiet when he was an infant. It was harder than watching him move away. It was nearly as tough a time as he had been through in Marian's last days. Roman spent the morning in the shop, puttering around the place, sweeping the floor, ordering the tools, and putting the finishing touches on the Laverda gas tank that Adam Steinberg had smashed with guilt and fury. Roman tried to do some work on a Ducati engine, but found he couldn't work his usual magic. The machine ran roughly. It made terrible sounds. He tinkered and adjusted and tinkered and adjusted, but he could not get it right. Finally he sat down heavily and wiped his brow with a shop rag. There was no way he could tune a bike. There was no way he could do anything but wait.

The rest of the day passed very slowly, and it was with great relief that he came out of the shop to the sound of Scooter's BMW in the driveway.

Biji waved. The sky was growing orange and the breeze was growing crisp. Scooter's saddlebags were full of clothes.

Biji gave Roman a big hug and Roman hugged her back. Scooter ambled into the shop and he stopped in front of the Laverda gas tank.

"Dad," he said with a frown as Roman and Biji walked through the door. Roman lifted his head.

"You painted this tank?"

Roman nodded.

"It's a Laverda tank, right?"

"You know a Laverda tank when you see one," said Roman.

"I know it shouldn't say 'Harley Davidson,' " said Scooter.

Roman walked over and surveyed the mess.

"Would you go and get us a couple of beers?" he said to Biji. He took out his wallet and offered her a five.

Nobody had ever asked Biji Steinberg to run out for a six-pack, but there was something in Roman's voice. Biji turned on her heel and walked out of the shop. Father and son watched her go. When she got outside she bent and let her hair fall to her knees, then she stood and shook it. She put her helmet down on the seat of Scooter's bike.

"We have to talk," said Roman.

"Shoot," said Scooter. He walked around to an ancient motorcycle that had been in the shop for as long as he could remember. Roman had always sworn he was trying to sell it, but Scooter knew he never would.

"Still run?" he asked his father.

"Serious talk," said Roman, ignoring the question.

Scooter put a leg over the bike. He moved it back and forth between his knees.

"You know what I did before I opened this place," said Roman.

"We don't have to talk about that," said Scooter.

"But we do."

"You don't do it anymore. It's in the past. Let's just forget it."

"You know I was very good," said Roman.

"I don't doubt it," said Scooter Loon.

"I mean I was *very* good."

"Okay."

"As good as you are with a bike. Maybe better."

"All right," said Scooter.

"But there was one thing I could never, ever do," said Roman. "One thing that I wanted to do more than anything in the whole wide world."

"You know, Dad, now is the time for that kind of thing. You should be enjoying your life. If you need some money or something . . ."

"I wanted to have a son," said Roman.

Scooter smiled at his dad. "Do you think I'm going to marry Biji? Is that what this is all about?"

"I stole more than jewels," said Roman.

The phone rang, but neither man moved to answer it.

"I don't think I want to hear any more," said Scooter.

"One time, many years ago, I had a VW microbus."

"I remember," said Scooter.

"One night, in the summer, I took my VW microbus and took a drive. I took a drive to Beverly Hills."

Scooter just stared.

"It was a warm night. There was a wind." Roman took a deep breath. "I took the bus because I wasn't coming back alone."

Scooter moved up over the kick starter and put his foot on the pedal. He stopped there, his body canted over, his arms locked up long and tight on the bars.

"I heard about this baby there, in Beverly Hills," said Roman.

"You took the bus to steal a baby?" said Scooter Loon. He kicked the old bike over. Smoke filled the shop.

"A very unusual baby. A baby I thought could get a hell of a grip on a drainpipe. A baby with a defect or two. A baby I was told nobody wanted."

Scooter Loon began playing furiously with the switches by the bars. He pulled the choke as far out as it would go. He jumped down on the pedal for all it was worth. He kicked the old engine into life and held open the throttle until it roared and roared and roared.